My Life With A Billionaire

Roger Williams

Also by Roger Williams

PETER THE GREAT

ISBN-13: 978-1-7343540-1-0

CHAPTER ONE

A Brief Encounter

I never dated a married man until I met Marc Gordon, although the "never" should be considered conditional because although he was technically still married, he'd been separated from his wife. (And because there are two "althoughs" in a single sentence, that should give you the hint I'm not a professional writer. Read on at your own risk.)

Marc was participating in an early-evening panel at the Stanford Law School about why so many founders of multi-billion dollar Silicon Valley companies were under thirty when they started their companies. After that they were usually toast as they rarely started a second successful company, much less a third or a fourth. (Of course, think Steve Jobs and Elon Musk as the exceptions to the rule.)

Marc was now thirty-three, having been forced out of his company by his partners and his VC backers on the grounds he was difficult to work with, which was true, BTW. Before starting his company, he had famously dropped out of Stanford's Computer Sciences grad school after just three days, claiming that he knew more about math and CS than any of his professors, so why should he be paying them to teach him. Also true, BTW. A couple of years later he partnered with two eventual backstabbing professors to form ByteAnalysis, a data-mining company, known colloquially in the Valley as "ByteMe." When the company went public a few years later, the IPO made him a multi-billionaire at the age of twenty-seven. The backstabbing came right after everyone had gotten very rich.

As a third-year law student, I attended this particular panel not because I had a serious interest in the sorry plight of over-the-hill tech founders; I was there because of Marc, who was known to be super-smart, quirky, rich and — full disclosure here — very good-looking. For that reason, there were more than the usual number of female students attending than would be normal for such a tech-heavy presentation. (No offense to the budding Ms. or Madame Curies out there. Just a fact.)

In his talk, Marc joked about how, in the opinion of some of his fellow panelists and the *cognoscenti* in Silicon Valley, he was washed up at thirty-three, past his prime, over-the-hill — pick your favorite cliché. Their collective conventional wisdom had decreed that Marc Gordon's entrepreneurial life was over. To that end, Marc had put together a PowerPoint which featured a few options about what he might do with the rest of his life. The first slide, "Kill Myself," was followed by a grainy black-and-white film of a rickety biplane attempting lift-off, but after being air-borne for just a few seconds, it did an immediate and inglorious nose-dive into the ground. In "Learn to Play a Musical Instrument," a burly, kilt-wearing Scotsman played a bagpipe while a dog lay on the ground and covered its ears. "Buy a Vineyard" featured shots of buxom peasant girls enthusiastically stomping grapes in wooden troughs. Well, you get the idea. And although he admitted he had no clue as to what might come next, he finished by saying, "I think I have at least one more start-up in me. Stay tuned...*la commedia non è finito*."

All he had to do was prove it.

Marc's presentation was followed by forty-five more minutes of tedious discussion as to why twenty-somethings were disproportionally successful in creating startups and washed-up thirty-somethings were not. Forty-somethings didn't even merit an honorable mention. This tiresome monotony was followed by another fifteen minutes of mostly inane comments and off-topic filibustering from the autodidacts in the audience.

When the event mercifully ended, I made my way down to where the panelists were chatting away with people from the audience, hoping to get in a few words with Marc, if you know what I mean, but the crowd of geeky guys and enthralled females surrounding him was too thick to penetrate. So...I headed off to the nearby parking garage, planning to join some friends for a quick dinner in Palo Alto before coming back and hitting the books for a couple of hours.

Outside, I was greeted by Northern California's brutal but normal February weather, which featured sheets of pelting rain, so I pulled the hood of my raincoat up tight around my head and walked quickly to my nearby dorm room, grabbed an umbrella and headed for the parking garage.

When I tried to start my ancient but usually-reliable Toyota, it wouldn't. I cranked the ignition key several times, but the engine just whirred and clicked. I got out, opened the hood and peered inside, not sure what I was looking for but hoping for a miracle, which arrived in the person of a Mr. Marc Gordon.

"Don't worry, I'm no Ted Bundy."

"You sure? You kind of look like him."

He laughed and said, "I'm not sure how to take that."

I said, "I know who you are. I was at the panel."

"What did you think?"

"It was...above-average, shall we say," I hedged, not willing to divulge my true feelings.

"Okay, so you didn't like it." He paused, then added, "What's your problem?"

"That's kind of personal, isn't it?"

He laughed again. "I mean, you've got the hood up and look very much like a damsel in distress, although judging from your attitude, I'd say there's not much actual distress involved."

"Oh, the car...it won't turn over."

He told me to try starting it again, which I did, but nothing happened. Just the clickety-click-clack of the solenoid trying to do its job.

"Try the lights."

I did and the beams were barely visible against the garage wall.

"I'm no expert, but I'd say you have a dead battery. If you had jumper cables we could probably get you going, but if it died, I wouldn't trust it to start again. Especially in this weather."

"Great."

"If you can leave it, I could drop you somewhere."

"I was planning on meeting some friends for dinner. Would San Francisco be too far?"

(Why did I say that? Why even a hint of snarkiness? Why push him away? It was a major personal failing — not letting anyone in.)

"I like to drive, but San Francisco might be that bridge too far."

"Actually, I'm meeting some friends in downtown Palo Alto. I was just plumbing the depths of your commitment."

So, I grabbed my purse, my umbrella and locked the car, not that anyone would, or even could, steal it in its current

4

state of inoperability. We walked down to the far end of the garage and got into his, a bright-red Tesla. Judging by how far we he had to walk and how empty was the garage, it was clear he had picked a place to park where no one was likely to give his Tesla an unintentional, or even an intentional, door-ding.

"I can see why you like to drive."

"I love this car. When I first got my IPO money I bought a Ferrari like everyone else, but when the Model S came out, I couldn't resist it. This was the fourth one off the line and it's simply better than any gas-powered car. And cheaper than the Italian jobs...relatively speaking, of course."

"And I'm sure you're saving a ton on gas."

He laughed. "Yeah, there's that too."

(Note to self: why do you have to be such a smart-ass?)

As we drove into town, he asked what I was planning on doing after law school and I told him I'd be taking the bar exam this summer and because I wasn't a gunner, the Supreme Court was not on my radar screen, so I'd be clerking for a federal appeals court judge in San Jose. For a year. After that, I told him I might then get a job working for the Antelope Rights Action Network or the Mountains Out of Molehills Legal Foundation.

"Those aren't actual organizations, are they?"

"Not really. It's just my way of saying I haven't made any long-term plans."

"You're funny," he said.

When we stopped in front of the restaurant I resisted the impulse to lean over and give him a peck on the cheek. Instead, I thanked him, we shook hands and I got out. My heart was beating at a somewhat higher rate than normal and I felt stirrings in places which had been dormant for most of law school.

I joined my friends for a Thai dinner and let them know I'd had a car problem and would need a ride back to campus. And because I didn't want to be seen as a star-struck, camp-following groupie, I didn't fill them in with the details of my very brief brush with fame. Instead, I just told them I'd gotten a lift from someone on the panel. No biggie.

My name is Cynthia Burrows, BTW.

CHAPTER TWO

Getting To Know You

After graduation and the bar exam, I started my clerkship in August for an appellate court judge in San Jose. His was one of the go-to venues for cases involving patents and copyrights, an area of the law I thought I was interested in, but after only a few weeks on the job, I just hoped I could make it through my clerkship year without embarrassing myself or dying of boredom. Dull as they were, estates, wills and trusts at least involved the human element. There were few such human interest stories in patent disputes between multi-billion dollar corporations and the patent-trolling lawyers who were trying to extort huge sums from said companies as compensation for their clients' minuscule contributions to a piece of software or a socially-worthless app. Basically, if the Apples and Googles of the world weren't making billions, there'd be no point in suing them. Think Willie Sutton.

I shared windowless chambers in the courthouse with a senior clerk and another fledgling law grad. Our judge, nearing retirement, was an early-bird and liked to get to work at six in the morning, but fortunately didn't expect his clerks to get there until eight, which was still early by appellate court standards, but was definitely early by law school standards where any professor who scheduled an eight o'clock was considered to be a fascist...a sadist...or both.

After the bar, I'd hooked up with a fellow Stanford Law grad to share an apartment in Mountain View. (Oops. Strike the "hooked up" part. What I mean to say was that we rented the apartment together and because he worked the usual first-year associate hours of ten to twelve a day for a firm in Palo Alto, we rarely saw each other.) Although not as bad as my roommate's, my workday was still a long one. I usually took the train down to San Jose because the traffic on the 101 Freeway was horrific and its only unpredictability was the degree of horrific-ness. So, after leaving at seven and getting home around the other seven, there was little time to do more than stop for some take out, watch an hour or so of TV and go to bed. Such was the exciting life of a young professional working at her first real job. At least there were plenty of decent and inexpensive restaurants nearby on Castro Street. Plus my law school loans were deferred until I left my clerkship and got a job that paid real money.

One day in late October, Mark called me at work. To say it was "out of the blue" would be a massive understatement; it was out of the galaxy. I hadn't thought about him in months. In fact, after a few days of our meeting, I didn't think about him at all. Of course, I wondered why he'd called after all this time, but when he asked me out, I, of course, said "yes," and because I didn't want to get too far out over my skis, I made it for a Thursday night, claiming I was busy on the weekend.

He picked me up his red Tesla, although, as it turned out, it was a new one, exactly the same as the old one, but with an upgraded battery pack it got sixty more miles on a full charge. Woo-hoo! Hence the trade in and so much for having a sentimental attachment to owning the fourth one off the line.

We went to a Michelin-starred Asian-fusion restaurant in Palo Alto. I'd heard about it while in law school, but even if I'd wanted to, there was no way I ever could have afforded the two-hundred fifty dollars per person *prix-fixe* dinner — not including drinks and wine.

Although I already knew a fair amount about him, we exchanged bits and pieces of our life stories over dinner. He asked a lot of questions and was a good listener, so I did most of the talking. Good seduction technique, BTW, the listening part — not that he would have needed any extra help in that department. However, I realized early on that I needed to keep my wits about me and not rush into anything. I would later mentally deconstruct the entire evening in detail.

In the course of the conversation, he told me he'd been separated from his wife for over a year and they were in the process of finalizing their divorce. They'd met when he was living in LA and enjoying the Drive-a-Ferrari/Date-a-Model lifestyle of a freshly-minted winner of an IPO jackpot. Shortly after they'd married and because he hated LA, they moved back to Palo Alto. With the divorce pending several years later, he split his time between Palo Alto and a beach house in Carmel while they remodeled a second house in Palo Alto for his soon-to-be ex-wife. When in Palo Alto, he lived in a cottage behind the main house in order to be close to his two kids. Of course, I'd Googled him before we went out and knew he and his wife had split up, but I didn't know the details of their his-and-her living arrangements. Strange, I thought, but I soon learned that this was just one of many things about Marc that were. (I also learned later that the "cottage," so-called, where he stayed while the divorce was pending was at least twice the size of any house I'd ever lived in.)

At one point I asked him, "Seeing that you seem to be

unemployed, what are your plans for getting a job?" He laughed and said he'd deal with that when his unemployment benefits ran out, then added, "If you're asking me what's next, the short answer is, 'I haven't a clue.'"

All in all, it was a good first date. We managed to slip into a comfortable back and forth with jokes about each other's fellow professionals — lawyers and techies. That the stereotypes of each profession bore only a passing resemblance to reality was of little importance to people like Marc and me who enjoyed a good laugh above all else. Unless, of course, someone had actually died. Then, out of respect for the recently-departed, we'd put the humor on hold. Briefly. Just sayin'.

Because it was a Thursday evening, I pled guilty to being employed and having to work the next day, so he drove me back to my apartment building and stopped out front. He started to get out to walk me up, but I told him I was pretty sure I could safely get to the door without his manly protection. I leaned over and gave him a quick kiss on the cheek and got out. And before closing the door, I leaned back in, shook his hand and told him I'd had a great time.

After he'd pulled away and was out of sight, I leaned back and sagged against the entryway wall. Several deep breaths later, I was okay. Had he walked me to the door, I wasn't sure I trusted myself enough to just say 'goodnight,' and that was definitely not the way I wanted our first date to end.

I had trouble getting to sleep that night, wondering, "why me?" To be perfectly honest, I'm reasonably good-looking but not a knock-out. I'm also smart, but am no genius, and here was a guy who could date practically anyone in the world and he'd asked me out. Before he drove off, he said he'd call, but we've all heard that before.

The next day I was worthless at work, but managed to bluff

my way through to five o'clock. I tried to concentrate, but random thoughts and fuzzy feelings about Marc kept popping up. I needed to sort all this out with someone, so I arranged to meet my friend and law-school classmate, Lizzy, and "Walk the Dish" in the hills behind the Stanford campus on Saturday morning.

The trail leading up to The Dish was a popular hiking route for Stanfordites as well as civilians from nearby towns. It was a "just right" hike for those in reasonable shape, but was difficult enough to discourage those who weren't. The trail started out just west of campus in the rolling grass-covered hills, now turned a deep yellow in the aptly-named Golden State's Indian Summer. (I'm not sure one can use that term nowadays, but I just did.)

The Dish was a radio telescope, although it was unclear to me whether it was meant to pick up radio signals from space aliens or if it was intended to actually scan the heavens for stars and galaxies. It resembled a clunky TV satellite receiver from the 1980's, and, seen from campus, looked to be the size of a toy from a Crackerjack box, but as you got closer, you realized how enormous it was as it stood tilted towards sky, a hundred and fifty feet across and nearly as high.

Because I now had the Marc genie sitting on my shoulder and was seeing everything with him in mind, I was pretty sure he'd know what The Dish was and would think it was stupid of me not to know. After all, I'd been hanging out around Stanford for four plus years and even someone with a mild sense of curiosity would have figured it out. The sad truth was I was now relating almost every thought I had about anything as to how I might talk about it with Marc, what he might think about it, etc., etc. It was sickening and it was driving me crazy. Was I back in high school?

As we walked, I filled Lizzy in about what had happened, and we spent the morning discussing the endless permutations of the date and where it might lead, should he ever call. This analysis carried over into a brunch/lunch at a cafe in Portola Valley. We first thought about getting something in Palo Alto, but I was terrified by the infinitesimally-minute possibility of running into Marc, something I definitely did not want to happen until I got a better fix on where I stood.

After listening to me deconstruct the date, my impressions, my feelings, my thoughts and my theories for several hours, Lizzy's basic advice was to "go for it."

The problem was...how, exactly, should I "go for it?" I didn't even have a Plan A, much less a Plan B.

Fortunately, I didn't have to figure that out.

Marc called. As promised.

CHAPTER THREE

I Meet The Kids

As an undergrad, I'd been in several relationships I thought were serious at the time. The most serious was with Brad. (Yes, a "Brad." Not his fault, BTW. I blame the parents.) We'd met in our senior year at college and it was my first relationship with long-term potential, but the whole West Coast-East Coast thing of my law school and his grad school proved to be too much to overcome.

Except for one rebound relationship, nothing serious happened in law school, mainly because I was just trying to keep my head above water.

While working at a couple of firms during the summers, I'd hit the bar scene a few times, but it was definitely not for me. And at each of those firms I had to fend off, carefully of course, advances by some of the associates who were my age as well as those by some of the partners who were definitely not my age.

So here I was, slaving away in the judges' chambers, meeting no one — not that you'd necessarily want to meet most of the people who hang out in and around a federal courthouse: convicted felons, soon-to-be convicted felons, their "business associates," defense attorneys, prosecutors and an assortment of similarly-unsavory types.

About my fellow cellmates, er...strike that...my fellow chamber-mates, one was a forty-something guy who fortunately had bought his Palo Alto two-bedroomer right out of law school and was now house-rich but cash-poor, as senior clerks barely made as much as first-year associates at the "Big Law" law firms. However, he did have the so-called prestige of working for a federal judge and I knew he was scheming to parlay that into a position somewhere else that paid real-world wages, what with two kids approaching college-age. My fellow junior clerk, Harvey Jacobson, was already on board for the second half of a two-year tour of duty. An obnoxious schemer and suck-up, he'd recently graduated from Hastings where he'd been a star, so his high opinion of himself and his legal skills were largely colored by the nature and quality of the pond in which he'd been spawned. Needless to say, we had little in common and hated each other. I was only three months into my year-long sentence and was already thinking about what to do next. (But, as an *obiter dictum*, "thinking about what to do next" was something I should have been doing regardless of how I felt about my clerkship. And, as a PS, I just threw in that *obiter dictum* because I know if Harvey ever reads this, he'll have to look it up. "Right, Harv?")

So, I was at loose ends career-wise and at a complete dead end, relationship-wise, which shouldn't be taken as evidence that I'd been totally cloistered away in a nunnery. I'd had a few casual coffee dates: a guy I'd met at the gym, another guy from my roommate's firm, and someone I'd met while standing in line one Saturday morning waiting for a chocolate croissant at the Mayfield Bakery, but none of these had gone or were ever going to go anywhere. Not that I was really looking, given my career-wise "loose ends," but if lightening were to strike...well, I was standing tall in an open field.

So when Marc called again, I was ready — for whatever. We'd talked a bit about modern art on our first date as I had always been interested in artsy stuff, but fortunately not enough to have majored in it. When he invited me to meet him at the Anderson Gallery on campus on a Saturday afternoon, I drove up from Mountain View and he rode his bike over from his place in Palo Alto. Because Stanford was playing Oregon in the football stadium later that afternoon, the eucalyptus grove in that part of campus was filling up with tailgaters getting ready for the Cardinals' big skirmish with the Ducks. Consequently we had the Gallery pretty much to ourselves. As it turned out, Marc was nearly as interested in the building's architecture as he was in its art, and he politely, but incessantly, quizzed an elderly docent to the point that to get rid of him she gave him the number of the gallery's head cheese, whom she said he could call the next week should he want more information, and, being as obsessively detail-oriented as he was, he probably did.

As we talked and wandered through the Gallery, there were light touches in both directions: wrists, forearms, shoulders, backs.

Standing in front of an enormous and impressive Jackson Pollack, Marc said, "It looks like a wiring diagram of the female brain."

I laughed but didn't take the bait. Instead, I threw him a line of my own, "If we can function as well as we do with an operating system like that, women should rule the world. Men's brains are like a Mondrian — all sharp edges and straight lines. No nuance."

"That's why we can get from Point A to Point B so quickly. No distractions."

"Then how do you deal with surprises?"

"There are always bumps in the road. We learn to ignore them."

"Oh, yeah. Then ignore this."

I turned and with both hands pulled his face down to mine and kissed him. Hard. On the lips while pressing my body up against his.

Sometimes I even surprise myself. It must be the way my female brain is wired.

Marc was taken aback but recovered quickly. "Okay. Point taken."

"I don't know exactly what's going on, but I thought I'd best get that out of the way. I hate uncertainty. Uncertainty and I don't get along."

After leaving the Anderson we walked over to the Rodin Garden and chatted as we wandered among the giant sculptures. Then, having had enough culture for the day, we sat on the patio overlooking the Rodins and drank hot teas, mine black with half-and-half and sugar and his a healthy green with no deleterious additions. After a half-hour or so of casual conversation, we ran out of things to say and sat there in a comfortable silence, soaking up what was left of the afternoon sun. We could hear the Stanford Band in the distance, warming up for the game. We didn't discuss "the kiss," and I made a point of not bringing up the whole relationship thing, whatever it was. Or wasn't.

As we were finishing our third refills, Marc said he had his kids that night and that he needed to get home soon. I told him if he needed help with some light cooking, I was available and would stay out of his way.

I could see him turning over the various options in his mind, but he quickly said "yes."

He gave me the address and I got there before he did. I parked, got out, and waited for him in front of a huge

16

wrought-iron gate, which gave me a chance to check out his crib. Looking like it probably enclosed an entire city block, a solid adobe wall stretched in both directions from the gate to the corners of the street. A tall hedge of privets fronted the wall, and with mounds of azaleas clumped in front of them, looked very much like the opening layout of a chess board with a line of pawns protectively-guarding a row of stately nobles. The lush greenery softened the Forbidden City aspect of the compound with the giant wall shielding the interior from the prying eyes of Google's StreetView, — or any other prying eyes for that matter.

When I walked over to the gate to peek inside, a burly man got out of a large black SUV parked down the street, leaned back against it and folded his arms. He pretended to be interested in something up in the sky, but was definitely keeping an eye on me. Because very few Palo Altans wore dark suits and ties in the afternoon, especially on a Saturday, I pegged him as a security guy, which was confirmed when Marc waved to him when he arrived.

As he pedaled towards me, Marc pointed a remote thingie at the gate and it swung open. He glided to a stop and we walked in together up a curved stone driveway to a modern Italian-style villa which was set at an angle to the street.

I tried to act nonchalant and not be impressed, but the house was stunningly gorgeous. My poor word skills can't do it justice, so I'll just go with the basics: two stories, red-tiled roof, a smooth pale-yellow stucco exterior now turning a deep gold in the late afternoon sun. Two giant steps up from the driveway and you were standing on a wide stone veranda in front of an antique wooden door so massive it looked like you'd need both hands to open it. The house was built around, or more accurately, under a canopy of giant live oaks, whose gnarly limbs twisted overhead like bony arthritic fingers. Strands of dry Spanish moss dangled from their branches and swayed in the breeze that gently wafted through them. Beneath the oaks, clumps of azaleas and rhododendrons, having long since shed their blossoms with the onset of fall, had settled in for the winter, conserving energy for their springtime blooming extravaganza.

We went inside and Marc was immediately swarmed over by his two kids, Ashley and Dion, ages seven and five, who were watched over by Teresa, a nanny. I found out later Teresa was one of a veritable army of nannies and was there for the weekend. With at least one nanny always on duty, keeping the Nanny Brigade at full strength was a priority for Marc and his ex-wife, Laura. Marc had mentioned that Laura lived in Palo Alto, but I didn't know then that she lived only four blocks away in a slightly-smaller but similarly-secure compound.

After we were all introduced, Dion pulled Marc away to show him something he'd made out of Legos, leaving me alone in the kitchen with Ashley, who apparently was in charge of making dinner. Wielding a giant chef's knife, I watched her cut and dice a shallot like a pro, curling the fingers of her left hand under to keep from nicking herself. I wondered about the wisdom of letting someone her age do what she was doing, but it clearly was not my place to express concern.

My cooking go-to was mac and cheese from a box, but here I was learning from a seven-year old that mac and cheese was better if you sautéed the chopped shallots in butter, added some flour and paprika, brought the roux to a boil, added milk, then cooled the sauce before adding grated cheddar and gruyère, thus avoiding a curdled mess. (Surprise! You didn't expect I'd throw a cooking lesson in here.) After adding the parboiled macaroni, into the oven it went with a breadcrumb topping.

"Did you learn this from your mom?" I asked.

"No, she can't cook either," she said, probably inadvertently referring to me. "From my dad."

Over the course of the next half-hour while Marc was occupied with Dion, I got a lot of good info from Ashley. The kids were only allowed to watch thirty minutes of TV a day. The same for computer games. No Facebook, no Twitter, no Instagram or Snapchat. Pretty strict, I thought, especially for a tech titan. Laura was a bit more lax (laxer?), but agreed in principle with the idea that kids could be creative without excessive computer use corroding their brains.

She also told me Laura's current live-in boyfriend was a motorcycle-riding, trumpet player who was fourth chair in the San Francisco Symphony. The kids spent most school-days with their mom, and even though Dion had just started kindergarten, both parents were heavily-involved with their schooling. One might think kindergarten would be fairly hands-off, but apparently not in the Gordon households. For a divorced couple, Laura and Marc got along reasonably well and apparently most disputes involved discipline levels for the kids. Needless to say, they never argued about money as Laura was well-taken-care-of.

Ashley was very relatable. I'd done a lot of babysitting in my day and preferred older kids to toddlers, especially those as verbally-adept as she. As she was spooning the mac and cheese into a baking dish, Ashley asked me, "Are you Dad's girlfriend?"

"No, honey. We're just getting to know each other." I had a feeling she'd almost said "new girlfriend," but caught herself.

After getting the mac and cheese into the oven, we then set about making creamed spinach, which was a surprise to me in that they liked it. My experience was that spinach in any form was pretty far down on most kids' food likability indices.

While the two of us continued working away in the

kitchen, Theresa sat at the dining room table, giggling as she texted back and forth with someone. From the way she was acting, I assumed it was a guy. It was also clear that she was not expected to help out with the dinner prep, a duty which Ashley had taken over.

We ate outside on the stone patio next to a huge swimming pool and looked across it to another vast array of azaleas and rhododendrons set beneath clusters of scarlet-leafed Japanese maples, which were protected by the enormous live oak canopy. The landscaping had a strong Asian bent and was worthy of Olmsted or Capability Brown. (OK, look 'em up.) The backyard would be spectacular in the spring and I wondered if I would be around to see it.

We'd just lost Daylight Savings Time the prior weekend, so by six it was getting dark — and chilly — even with patio heat lamps glowing above us. We retreated to the kitchen for a store-bought dessert: Häagen-Dazs ice cream and apple tarts from Trader Joe's. Apparently there was a limit on how much was expected from a seven-year old chef, no matter how talented.

As it turned out, however, both kids were expected to clean up after dinner. I started to help out but Marc signaled me not to. They cleared the table and Ashley directed the loading of the dishwasher. There was supposed to be no whining, but a squabble broke out when Ashley felt that Dion was dragging his feet. She insisted she'd done way more than her half and was not about to do Dion's half as well. Besides, she argued, she'd made the mac and cheese and the spinach. Dion pouted, but picked up his pace and in the end, did his share of the cleanup. I was glad to see a bit of imperfect normality creep into the family dynamic.

By seven it was pitch-black when Marc walked me out.

"I'd ask you to stay but I've got the kids."

"Thanks for a wonderful afternoon...and evening." I paused before adding, "I love your kids."

We looked at each other for a few seconds before he kissed me. For real this time.

"Next weekend?" he asked.

"Sounds great."

"I'll call you."

He hit a button by the front door and the front gate swung open. I got into my trusty old Corolla and made my re-entry into the real world as I drove down Alma Street to my decidedly non-ritzy Mountain View apartment.

CHAPTER FOUR

It Happens

I was forced to scuttle our plans for the following weekend because my judge had reshuffled his calendar, which meant my fellow judicial minions and I were going to have to put in a bunch of extra hours. The judge claimed we hadn't been working as hard as we should have and we needed to pick up the pace; however, the senior clerk later dropped the news that the judge had been asked to give a couple of lectures at a legal retreat in early December — on Maui. All expenses paid, of course. Life at the top was hard. After wrapping up that grueling undertaking, he would then take some (ahem... sarcasm alert) well-deserved vacation time traveling around the Islands. To outsiders, he was a witty raconteur who charmed juries and the general public with his jokes and insider stories about bad behavior by the attorneys and the perps who appeared before him, but to his clerks, he was a hard-taskmaster (no fault with that), except that the ratio of criticism to praise broke heavily in favor of the former.

So instead, Marc invited me to spend Thanksgiving Weekend with him in Carmel, although Turkey Day itself was reserved for time with his kids. Implied but unspoken was that this would be the weekend when It..would happen.

I spent Thanksgiving Day with some married law school friends, but didn't tell them how I was planning to spend the rest of the weekend.

Marc picked me up on Black Friday and we drove down to his place on the beach south of town. (At the time I wondered about exactly how many places he had. As it turned out, not that many, but in retrospect, I was glad he had this one.)

We parked, carried our luggage in and…It…Happened.

Fast.

I'm not one to go into all the not-so-gory details, but Black Friday it wasn't. More like the Fourth of July.

Afterwards, I took a nap, then a shower; or maybe it was a shower, then a nap. I don't now remember the exact order of things. At any rate, after I woke up I found a note Marc had left letting me know he'd gone for a walk on the beach. This gave me time to explore the house by myself.

It stood on a rocky bluff overlooking the Pacific and came with the usual fancy beach house stuff: kitchen, huge living room, fireplace, TV room, probably four bedrooms with the master facing the ocean. Style-wise, it was very guy-ish, with lots of glass and steel and a color scheme of subdued shades of blues and grays. With thick floor-to-ceiling glass walls facing the Pacific, one could leave any room on the ocean side and walk out onto the cantilevered deck which hung suspended high above the breaking waves below. Outside, a narrow path down to the beach wound through mounds of sand and moss-covered rocks which poked their heads up through thick clusters of ice plant. The shore itself was more rock than sand, and off to the south was a huge granite outcropping that marked the end of the beach and gave Marc's place a feeling of near-total privacy.

After completing my self-guided tour, I made some tea and curled up in front of the electric fireplace with a Jane

Austin novel I'd decided to re-read. Cozy.

By the time Marc returned from his walk, the sun was setting behind the fog bank which hovered on the horizon. A drizzly grey mist was now wafting up over the incoming waves, which seemed to be rising. I assumed it was the tide, but growing up as a desert rat in Arizona, I didn't really know. Marc kissed me and said he needed to spend some time working on something he'd been thinking about. I went back to my Jane while he headed off to his man-cave. Of course, it wasn't actually a "cave," but more of an office/den-type room which, like almost every other room in the house, looked out over the Pacific.

After what seemed to be a couple of hours but was probably just one, Marc resurfaced and I asked him what he'd been doing.

"Working on some things I've been thinking about."

"Such as?"

"I can't talk about it. Talking about it gets in the way."

"Okay," I told him. I got it — non-communication in that area came with the territory.

About Marc, one could say, "Genius at work" without irony.

What came next, you might ask? Well, dinner for one thing. Then the other thing again before we went to sleep. That pretty much summed up the weekend. Food. Sex. Brief walks on the beach. Then Marc back onto his computer or him standing out on the deck staring out at the ocean, thinking about...well...who knew? I certainly didn't. In addition to reading Jane, I'd brought my laptop and was glad to be able to get some work done.

We did leave the house twice on Saturday and both excursions were food-oriented: first for lunch and then for a late dinner. For the whole weekend the weather was overcast, cold and breezy — much too unpleasant to spend much time outside. However, after the lunch we did manage to slip in a little window-shopping in Carmel, with an emphasis on "a little," as Marc was clearly uninterested, but tolerated it. So I didn't push it, as heavy-duty shopping wasn't really my thing either.

We drove back late Sunday when the traffic was light and planned to get together the next weekend. Speaking for myself, I could say "Mission Accomplished," not that I'd actually had such a specific mission in mind. (Ha-ha! I'm sure if you've made it this far, you're not likely to be a member of the credulous crew who would believe such rubbish.)

CHAPTER FIVE

Happy Holidays

After Thanksgiving it was a short sprint to Christmas, during which time we had a couple of weekday restaurant dinners and one Saturday night date which ended with my staying over.

We talked about a lot of things but assiduously avoided any discussion about "the relationship." I had the intuitive sense he was not the kind of guy who was willing to take that deep dive into the minutiae of feelings, emotions, etc. (Not that there were many guys who were comfortable exploring that territory, and those who were, contrary to popular opinion, weren't all that interesting, at least to *moi*.) I was pretty sure that he would see such a discussion as a way for him to end up in a corner he didn't want to be backed into. As for me, I was comfortable with the *status quo*, at least for now and for the foreseeable future.

We did talk about our Christmas plans. Other than popping down to Arizona to spend a couple of days with my mom and my sister's family, I had none worth mentioning. For his part, Marc was taking the kids to Maui along with Laura and her mom, but minus the trumpet-playing, Harley-riding boyfriend. For a divorced couple, they were pretty tight, but there were limits, and for now, one would be not spending a vacation with either of the other's new "Friend with Benefits." I was beginning to realize that nearly everything about Marc didn't fit into the common understanding of what would be considered normal.

So, for Christmas I flew down to Arizona and took a SuperShuttle out to Surprise, my old hometown, where I'd gone to school from kindergarten through twelfth grade. (And please, no jokes about the name. As kids, when asked where we were from, we would sometimes wave our arms and shout, "Surprise!" However, by the time we got to high school, it had stopped being cute. Not to mention old.)

My mom couldn't pick me up when I flew in because she was working a shift at her hospital and my sister was busy with her two kids, so taking a SuperShuttle the thirty miles out from Sky Harbor was my best option. The cost of a taxi or even an Uber would have been astronomical, and financially, I was still living on my own dime.

Surprise was always the last stop for a shared ride on a SuperShuttle, and one of the small joys I got from taking it was in checking out the incongruous holiday decorations as we rolled through Geezerville, formally known as Sun City, where one would see blinking Christmas lights strung around giant saguaros, teams of inflated reindeer and sleighs resting on glistening white gravel, mall Santas in Bermuda shorts…well, you get the idea…tasteful, it was not. Still, I was glad to see the old Xmas spirit was still strong among the senior set.

When I arrived at my mom's, I used the code and let myself in through the garage. I found a note in the kitchen saying she'd left a lemon meringue pie, my fave, in the fridge. I sampled it immediately and… 'twas delish. Because she cooked like me and *vice versa*, I knew she hadn't baked it herself, so I rummaged through the trash and found the

Marie Callender box it had come in — a noteworthy little factoid which I filed away for future reference.

I parked my suitcase in my old bedroom, which hadn't changed since I'd headed off to college nearly a decade ago. I found Mollie, the calico, curled up on the living room sofa. Looking for something to do, she followed me as I poked around the house, checking out the changes. There weren't many.

My mom's place was a stuccoed rancher with a tiled roof, three bedrooms, two baths, a small office and a lanai that opened out to a swimming pool which could be covered in two strokes. A lap pool it was not, but it was great for cooling off in July when it was a hundred and ten in the shade and you didn't want to know how hot it was in the sun.

My family, such as it was, had its own quirky nature. Despite a poor marriage with years of mistreatment before, during and after, my mom still kept in touch with my dad. They met when she'd just started her career as a resident nurse in gerontology and he was a rep for a medical equipment company — one of his many career choices that ended up in the dumpster. Slightly older than my mom, my dad was a charismatic natural-born, life-long grifter/hustler who was always working on a new scheme which was bound to make him rich. They divorced when I was seven and my sister nine, and because my mom felt we should have a male role-model in our lives, he would show up at school plays, graduations and other events where he would mix and mingle with the other parents and take credit for my and my sister's various accomplishments, despite having contributed exactly nothing to them.

After going off to college, I had little to do with him other than the perfunctory call or card on birthdays. After my mom divorced him, he married twice and started families with each of his new wives. I was not in the least interested in finding out anything about my much younger half-siblings other than to feel sorry for them. However, what with me being a reasonably empathetic person, IMHO, you would be right in presuming I had an ongoing guilt overhang about this. After the divorce, my mom had several short-term relationships but none that went the distance. Now in her fifties, she was clearly resigned to living a single's life. Too many bad experiences had taught her that her judgement in the Man Department was not the best. Sometimes what you learn from your parents is not to repeat their mistakes, and I hoped I would not follow her path.

When she came home from her shift at the hospital, she asked the usual questions: how was my job? was I seeing anyone? To which I said, "Yes, I'd just started dating someone," but I was vague about the specifics. Saying "He's in tech," was as far as I was willing to go. If there was one skill I'd mastered in law school, it was the ability to deflect unwanted questions.

Although I loved my mom, she had a way of giving relationship advice I didn't want, especially considering her previous disastrous relationships with men.

The next day, Xmas Eve, she was working another day shift at the hospital, so I dropped her off and spent the morning just driving around, checking out some my old haunts. Before coming down, I'd emailed several friends about getting together for lunch, but they'd either begged off, citing general busyness, or weren't going to be around. Now ten years out from high school, I realized I was losing my connection to the place where I'd grown up. I had my memories…of people, places and events, but they were from a time in my life that was slowly receding into the past, displaced by a more interesting and exciting present.

Some people have a visceral connection to the place they

grew up, but I never did. All my life I'd wanted to get away from the desert and its unbearable summer sun which administered a merciless beat-down every second you were outside. Still, I felt a little depressed about my growing disconnectedness and the fact that I was missing something other people had. I was also beginning to realize I would not be coming back that often, which was sad. Nor would I miss not coming back, which was also sad.

We spent Christmas Eve at my sister's. She was the only halfway-decent cook amongst the three of us, but she had the usual issues carnivores had with my vegetarianism. She always wanted to make something special for me, but wasn't able to manage more that the typical holiday go-to of yams topped with marshmallows, even though I was fine with that, BTW. Her two kids, strangely enough, were the same ages as Marc's, five and seven, but weren't nearly as precocious, which was just one more thing that made me sad. My sister's husband, Fred, was a nice guy, but had it been Thanksgiving instead of Christmas, he would have been happily hunkered down in front of the TV watching football all day. Not that I was setting the world on fire, but as I saw my sister's dreams fade and her horizons shrink, I realized how ordinary her life seemed.

I flew back late on Christmas Day. One travel secret I'll share is that on the actual holiday everyone travels for, planes are only half-full at best. So it was an easy, uncrowded, two-hour hop-skip-and-jump back to San Jose. With the judge and everyone else out of the office for the gap week between Christmas and New Year's, I put in a few solo days at work and then went over to Marc's to celebrate New Year's Eve. It was the first time I'd had an official invite, so I packed an overnight case and was determined not to leave anything: a sweater, socks, undies — any item that would even hint at a surreptitious marking of territory.

If you're a party animal, you can skip the next part.

New Year's Eve was huge: a veritable excitement extravaganza! We interrupted a Netflix movie at nine to watch the ball drop in Times Square , finished the movie and went to bed around eleven. No staying up 'til midnight for us. Before heading over for the "festivities," Marc warned me that "going out" was not on the agenda. I wasn't much of a party gal myself, but left to my own devices, I probably would have stayed up until midnight and maybe shared some champagne with a few friends. Any thought I'd had that Marc led a Gatsbyesque life of excitement and glamour had long been put to rest. "I'm not crazy about socializing," he once told me. No kidding.

Christmas and kids' birthdays were a different matter. "Kids deserve whatever you can give them. Childhood ends soon enough." I wasn't sure what he meant by that. Did it reflect something about his own upbringing? (A little foreshadowing here — next Christmas I would find out.)

CHAPTER SIX

The Proposition

We didn't see much of each other during the first few weeks after the holidays. Marc flew back east to check out some potential investments and I needed to re-engage with my job. The judge was finally back from his Hawaiian boondoggle (thanks, taxpayers) and his extensive island-hopping Xmas vacation, and because he felt he was behind, we were deemed to be officially behind, so there was some serious catching up to do. (We weren't really behind, BTW, but as all worker bees know, it's the misperception in the boss's mind that counts.)

And *pour moi*, it was also getting to be well past time to figure out what lay beyond the end of my clerkship because I would be one and done at the end of August. In the legal world, you generally don't give two weeks notice and expect to start a new job right away without having done some serious legwork beforehand, and obviously my situation was complicated by the uncertainty of my relationship with Marc. I kinda, sorta needed to know where we stood, because I had a long-standing offer from a DC firm which I would have to accept or reject pretty soon. Or find something else. Were Marc and I going to continue on with our relationship as an ongoing casual hook-up, or was there more to it than that?

The big issue for me was how to bring this up without causing "A Major Disturbance in the Force."

When Marc got back from the East Coast he asked me to come down to Carmel with him on Super Bowl Weekend. (And no, it's not a grammatical error to say "on Super Bowl Weekend" instead of "for Super Bowl Weekend," because in his invite he didn't mention the Super Bowl, he just said "… for the weekend," which just happened to be the weekend we celebrated our country's unofficial national holiday.) The Super Bowl was of no interest to him, and unless Tom Brady was playing, I wasn't interested in it either, other than the fact that it was a chance to hang out with friends and share some food and wine.

I had plans, but cancelled them and we drove down late Saturday morning. A major winter storm was already barreling in off the Pacific, and when we turned west at Salinas, it was delivering biblical proportions of pelting rain up and down the coast. When we turned south onto the Pacific Coast Highway, huge torrents of water swirled across the road in front of us, and the wind, coming in off the ocean, hit the Tesla with such force that the side windows could have used industrial-grade windshield wipers. Most unpleasant.

Knowing bad weather was on the way when he called, I asked him, "Why this weekend?" and he told me it was to watch the waves. Big waves was a thing with him and the bigger the better. He had studied the ocean currents, tide tables, the moon, the sun, the stars, the…well, all the variables that might affect wave-size and he'd determined Super Bowl weekend was going to be wave-watching prime time. It wasn't all original research, BTW, because, as you might suspect, there was a website for every goofy obsession known to man. (And yes, "known to man" is the appropriate term in this case, because women usually don't go in for that sort of thing.)

Having survived the mini-typhoon on our trip down, we finally arrived at the beach house in late afternoon. I noticed that since we were last here on Thanksgiving weekend, the house next door had disappeared. I asked him what had happened to it and he said, "I think a big storm took it out." When I seemed skeptical, he laughed and said, "I got tired of looking at it, so I bought it and had it torn down."

"So you made them an offer they couldn't refuse?

"Something like that."

"Okay..." I thought, "...for a vacant lot, ten to twenty million dollars just went to money heaven."

After settling in, we donned yellow New England rain slickers and ventured out onto the deck. Me carefully and Marc not so much. The waves were terrifying. And exhilarating. I hung onto the railing for dear life as the waves thundered and crashed against the rocks below, sending up huge plumes of water that soared into the air around us and doused the deck with spray. Supported as it was by concrete pillars as thick as Iowa grain silos, the house did not budge, although the inch-thick glass walls did shudder in the wind. But obviously Marc was not worried, so I was not worried... okay...some. Maybe more than a little.

After a while I retreated into the safety of the house for a warm shower and a hot toddy. Marc stayed out on the deck until the sun set and night fell, leaving the waves to crash below us on their own in the darkness. I wondered what he'd been thinking about as he stood out there staring at the waves. Moby Dick? Captain Ahab? I hoped he was not imagining himself standing like Leo at the prow of the Titanic, muttering to himself that famous "I'm king of the world" line.

We ordered dinner in, which was brought to us by a thoroughly-wet and clearly-unhappy delivery guy who had his mood brightened by Marc's very generous tip.

Around midnight the power went out up and down the coast, but...'twas not a problem for us. Of course forward-thinking Marc had that contingency covered; he fired up a basement generator and with power restored, everything started humming again. In addition to keeping us cozy and safe, we performed our good deed for the day, or in this case for the night, by impersonating a lighthouse, warning any crazy, deranged mariners still at sea to steer clear.

I slept in the next morning while Marc busied himself as usual on his massive computer setup, which, down to the last desktop icon, was identical down to the one he had at home. Something to do with "mirroring," which I didn't understand.

The next set of big waves were supposed to hit in late-afternoon, but when it became clear they wouldn't reach the level of Saturday's terrifying onslaught, we decided to head home early, but a quick online check of the traffic suggested we'd best wait until early evening.

Instead of settling in at the beach house and maybe watch a bit of the Super Bowl, we packed up and headed out for a very Early Bird dinner at a local Italian place Marc liked. Even at this fairly high-end restaurant, most of the patrons were watching the game on a TV in the bar, so we found a quiet table away from the action and ordered dinner.

I decided this was as good time as any to bring up the subject of what I should do after my clerkship ended. I began by tossing out a couple of options: work for a non-profit, try to land a research fellowship at the law school, and I ended my opening statement with the possibility of taking the DC job.

I was unprepared for Marc's response: he immediately leapt into problem-solving mode in what essentially amounted to a vigorous cross-examination of the witness, namely *moi*. What were the pros and cons of each option? What kind of work did I like? What were my long-erm goals?

Although I'd mentioned to him several times before that my clerkship would be ending in the fall, it was clear the implications of that decision hadn't registered with him at all. It was as if he realized for the first time that what I might decide to do next in my life would disrupt his. For someone who was so perceptive about many things, he was myopic on this topic. (Sorry about the rhyming; it's something I should work on.) The fact that he'd been able to entirely ignore this was part of the tunnel vision which had made him successful in other, non-relationship areas. That would be the kind way of putting it. Calling it extreme narcissism would be the less kind way. As to which was more accurate...I vacillated.

In the course of our back and forth, he offered to call his Palo Alto firm and have them take me on. That, however, was a Big No for me, as it would be obvious to everyone that I'd gotten the job through him, and although I knew this was often the way of the world, I didn't want it to be my way.

When I realized he hadn't given this much, if any, thought, I purposefully didn't bring up the fact that at some point I would have to start paying down my law school loans. I was afraid he would offer to pay them off — pocket change to him, but real money to me — because I would have felt like... well...to put it bluntly, a kept woman.

I quickly realized that bringing up this issue had touched off a flood of thoughts and feelings he clearly was having trouble dealing with. I wasn't sure he was even aware of how on edge he was. Introspection, especially about relationships, was not a big part of his makeup.

The drive back was uncomfortable, and because it was

also dark, raining hard, and the traffic was still heavy, Marc had to concentrate on driving. We made a bit of small talk in between long silences, but it was clear that our discussion about my future had indeed caused what I'd feared — a serious "Disturbance in the Force." How great was the perturbation? TBD.

He dropped me off at my apartment and offered to help with my small suitcase, but I waved him off. We hugged and there was a perfunctory kiss goodbye.

Given his unsettled state of mind, I wasn't sure when, or even if, we'd be seeing each other again.

The next two weeks were hell. I wasn't depressed, but I did walk around with a constant knot in the pit of my stomach. Sleeping was tough and the situation was wearing me down, but I was determined not to call, text, email or check in with him in any way. "Whatever happened to female empowerment?" you might ask. You could argue that I had a right to know how we stood with each other, but I had the sense that any attempt to discuss, claim, or insist upon "my right to know" might send him running in the opposite direction — if it hadn't already.

But finally, he called. He wanted to meet on a Saturday morning at one of his favorite hangouts, the Mayfield Bakery in the Town And Country shopping center. Ten o'clock. The fact that he'd chosen what was neutral territory put me on high alert. I was prepared for the worst.

Saturday came and it was one of those sunny and warm February mornings in California that lulled one into thinking Spring had sprung, but the reality was the Ides of March was only a few weeks away, lurking and ready to wreak its havoc.

The cafe was busy and he was uncharacteristically late. He showed up on his bike and gave me a perfunctory hug. He was clearly nervous and I expected the hammer to drop.

After getting coffee and croissants, we sat down at an outside table, and without hesitation, he told me he wanted me to move in with him.

To say I was completely floored would be the biggest understatement of my twenty-seven-year life. I was totally... completely...surprised.

But being the impulsive kind of person I was, I stood up, walked around the table, leaned over and kissed him. Hard. In front of everyone. Then without a word, I sat back down in my chair and with trembling hands tore apart my chocolate croissant.

"Well, I guess that's settled," he said.

We spent the rest of the day at his house. And after doing it, we talked about the what, when and where of living together, but not about the why. I was pretty sure that any statements like, "I love you," or even, "I like being with you," would not be forthcoming. I also felt I could not talk to him about it as his likely response would be something along the lines of "I wanted to," or "It seemed like a good idea," and for him, that would have been explanation enough. Anything more would be seen as fishing for a compliment or asking for a reason when it was obvious that no discussion was needed, at least in his mind. I was also aware of the old saying about not poking the bear unless one was prepared to deal with the likely negative consequences. I suspected that from his point of view, the fact that he wanted me to move in was proof enough about how he felt — and for me, it was.

Over the next months I would many times wonder, "Why me?" (And yes, I know there are those out there who would think, "Why not me?" but I wasn't a member of the group born with such self-assurance.) What did he see in me that prompted him to invite me into my life? On my end, there were no such questions about "why him?"

That question would linger in the back of my mind for a long time, but let me put it aside for now and talk about logistics. We'd have separate bedrooms, although having separate bedrooms in Marc's house was like having separate presidential suites at the Ritz. What did mine have? En- suite bath? Check. Glassed-in shower? Check. Tub the size of Lake Tahoe? Check. Walk-in closet the size of…well, you get the idea. My meagre collection of clothes would have felt lonely in even the smaller of the two walk-ins.

The bedrooms were on the same floor — the second. I did wonder if I was the first live-in occupant not-named Laura, but I was also pretty sure I didn't want to know the answer. It was a comfort that Marc told me I could change anything I wanted in my room. Just figure it out, order whatever I wanted and have it done. That was enough to make any woman's heart go pitter-patter. (And for once I kept my mouth shut. No need to go all snarky in the face of such generosity by blurting out something like, "how about a bathroom mirror lined with fake mink fur?")

The truth was that not much needed changing, although at some point I was fairly certain I'd feel the need to put my personal stamp on things, but because I wasn't a natural in the interior decorating department, I figured I'd wait until inspiration struck.

We toured the house, but having already stayed over several nights, there was not much about the overall layout I didn't already know. But, just FYI, it had all the usual rich guy accessories: wine cellar, workout room, bedrooms too numerous to count, separate guest house, etc., etc. The kitchen, however, was his pride and joy. It featured two gigantic built-in refrigerators, a separate freezer and a third fridge in the pantry, a wine closet with a wine cooler, an eight-burner gas stove, two ovens, blenders, mixers, expresso machines and even a blast chiller. You name it, he had it.

The security room was one I hadn't seen before. Located near Marc's bedroom, a bank of monitors displayed video from the several dozen cameras which covered every inch of the property. Later that afternoon, Marc had Cliff, the head security guy, come over and give me a rundown of phone numbers, codes, cameras, visitor protocols — mainly to make sure neither I nor any of my friends could be mistaken for an intruder who needed to be taken down or taken out by one of his goons.

Cliff's team also had an off-site place where they monitored the outside cameras for Mark and Laura as well as other clients. The inside cameras were strictly his and hers. And because we lived on a public street on which any lowlife could drive up and down, one of Cliff's guys was parked out on the street near each house 24/7. I found out later that when Marc and Laura first moved in, there'd been a kerfuffle with a couple of the neighbors who complained to the city about the fact that a security guy was parked on the street at all times, but one of Marc's lawyers eventually convinced them that it was actually a net positive — spillover private security for free. Given the level of intelligence needed to come to that conclusion, I had to wonder about some of my new neighbors.

In between the tour and the logistics briefing, I did manage to squeeze in a few words about my future plans. I made it clear that I wanted to continue with my legal career, although how that would play out was the great unknown. Marc said he'd thought it over and would back any decision I decided to make. It was totally my call. He'd help, of course, if I wanted it.

With that settled and logistics taken care of, we ordered dinner in and I spent the night, although spending that first night in my own room would have to wait.

On Sunday I drove down to Mountain View and picked up a couple of week's worth of supplies. I talked with my roommate and told him I would pay my share of the rent until the lease ran out in August. He was free to have the place to himself until then, but I made it clear I might want to move back in at a moment's notice. I realized I might be walking a tightrope with Marc and I wanted to have a safety net below, just in case. I had only lived with one other guy — it lasted two months and didn't end well.

CHAPTER SEVEN

The Daily Grind

After a few months, our life together settled into a comfortable routine. I would leave early, take the train from the California Avenue station to San Jose, put in my eight to ten hours, and come home. Marc would usually cook something or order take out. We'd watch a little TV and I'd go to bed.

Some mornings I'd leave early and hit the gym before Marc was up, or he'd leave first and take off on a long bike ride if the weather was good, and this being California, it mostly was. Cooking was his responsibility and unlike *moi*, he was not the type to open the fridge fifteen minutes before dinner-time to figure out what to make. Or microwave something (my *modus*, BTW.) He often planned meals a couple of days ahead, but always checked in with me before making the final call. We'd try to go out at least one night a week, usually on a Thursday or on a Saturday if we didn't have the kids. Friday nights were reserved for pizza and a movie — at home. Kind of a in-house date night for a steady couple. And by Friday, this still-working gal was more than ready to stay in and recuperate.

Weekends were reserved for adventures with the kids. He,

or I could now say, "we," got the kids every other weekend, and about once a month Marc planned a kid-friendly outing: an overnight in Carmel with a tour of the Monterey Bay Aquarium, a museum visit, or a trip up to the Exploratorium in San Francisco — their fave.

Early on, one of these day trips involved an afternoon of sailing on the San Francisco Bay. We drove up to the marina and took a fifty-five footer out for a spin, or whatever is the operative term for a boat ride. Marc didn't own the sailboat and didn't want to. "Nothing but a money pit," said the billionaire. (In some ways he was extremely money-conscious, or in the vernacular, "cheap.") However, he loved sailing and the rougher the seas, the better, but with two young kids on board, in the interests of safety he had a standing arrangement with "his guy, Mike," who owned the boat. Mike knew what he was doing, took no risks, and as a consequence always had at least two other guys on board, just in case.

I only "went to sea" once. As someone who could get sick just looking at a ferris wheel, I discovered right away that sailing wasn't *pour moi*. Much to Ashley and Dion's amusement, I spent my maiden, and only, voyage hanging onto the rail and throwing up over the side.

Afterwards, Marc told me, "It looks like you can take sailing off your bucket list."

I replied, "Forget the list. What I really needed was a bucket."

On subsequent sailing adventures, I would bid them *bon voyage* and either hang out at home in Palo Alto or play the landlubber by visiting friends in SF or just go shopping, then join the rest of the gang for dinner at a kid-friendly restaurant.

On our third week of living together, I met Laura. It was

her weekend with the kids, but the nanny on-duty came down with something at the last minute, and because Laura and her motorcycle-riding, trumpet-playing boyfriend had plans for the evening, we did the babysitting honors. How did it go? (The meeting, that is, not the baby-sitting.) Well, she was polite, but cool in the same way a glacier is cool — cold and permanently icy. I doubted we'd be having lunch anytime soon.

I found out later one of the conditions of the divorce was if she wanted to share the kids, she would have to live in Palo Alto until they finished high school, and if she moved earlier, the support agreement would be revised downward — dramatically. Nor would she have the kids. I thought perhaps her lawyers had not served her well, but after living with Marc for even a short time, I realized he could be incredibly stubborn, and had she insisted on living elsewhere, it would have been a serious deal-modifier, if not a deal-breaker. And because Marc had made his big money before they married, I was fairly sure the pre-nup was pretty tight. On the other hand, unless you were in Paris or London, having to live in Palo Alto wasn't like living in…well, no need to name names here. I'm sure you know what I mean.

I'm guessing here, but Marc's hermit-like life-style was probably the main point of contention that led to their divorce. He'd met Laura in L.A. during the brief period in his life when he was dating models and actresses, and she was from that world, an aspiring thespian hoping for a career in show biz. However, having graduated *cum laude* from Yale definitely separated her from the other actress/starlet wannabes, and because she was smart as a whip, it was only natural that she and Marc hit it off. That, coupled with her understanding of show-biz and the long odds of success, led her to have a wider range of interests than just getting an acting gig on a sitcom. And because she was way more outgoing and gregarious than Marc, she wanted more of a social life and a greater involvement in cultural things. And travel. In short, normal stuff. In that respect, Marc and I were a good fit because I didn't need a busy social life; however, I was hardly the recluse he was.

After they'd married and moved to Palo Alto, the arrivals of Ashley and Dion put a serious crimp in her acting career. However, she still occasionally spent a few days auditioning in LA, mainly just for the heck of it, because at thirty-four she knew it was getting to be a bit late in the game to believe The Big Break was just around the corner. And even being Marc Gordon's ex wasn't much help in La-La-Land, a world filled with the good-looking ex-wives of rich guys. Even so, I had to admit she was still very attractive, which was not something I cared to think about, because, comparatively, I was clearly running in second place in the looks department, which did make me nervous at times.

With her house just four blocks away, one day soon after moving in I drove by to take a peek. Hoping not to be recognized, I scrunched down so far in my old Toyota that a passerby might have thought the car was driving itself. Like Marc's, her house was surrounded by a high wall that blocked any look-see from the street, but unlike Marc's, hers only took up half a block. Because I was unlikely be invited in anytime soon — if ever, I'd have to depend on pics from Ashley and Dion to give me a sense of what I was up against. As I neared the end of her property, one of the security guys who was drinking a cup of coffee while leaning up against his car, waved to me as I drove by. I hoped he wouldn't rat me out, although, dammit, because it was a city street and open to the public, I had every right to be there.

Despite the fact that they were divorced, I got the sense that Laura felt she should have some say in Marc's choices in girlfriends. And after meeting her, I got the distinct impression she didn't think I'd last, that I was simply a bit player who would surely soon be easily-replaced. Even though I had doubts about the longevity of our relationship, I made it one of my goals to get past Spring Training and make it to Opening Day, just to prove her wrong. Still, I had to give her credit for being a good mom, although I found I could hate her for that as well.

Contradictory?

Yes.

True?

Also yes.

Don't say I'm not complicated.

Given that Marc was someone considered to be "highly eligible" and because he could pretty much have his pick of anyone in the field of eligible women, you might be wondering what the attraction was between us. It was an easy answer on my part: he was obviously intelligent, good-looking, considerate (well, fairly-considerate) and came with no major negativoes. Then "why me," one might ask? I'm reasonably attractive, if I say so myself, but not one with movie-star looks. My thinking on the matter was, and is, that Marc had normal needs, but didn't like the shrapnel that came with many relationships, as it had in his marriage to Laura.

How would you characterize someone who didn't go clubbing? Didn't over-indulge in alcohol? Liked to stay home on weekends and watch Netflix? If the first word you thought of was "frumpy," you wouldn't be far off, and I would only be slightly-offended by that (well, maybe a bit more than "slightly.") I was, and still am, a homebody. In short, I was low maintenance.

However, I realized Marc needed a woman in his life and if it weren't me, it would be someone else, and it would probably be someone pretty much like me. I wasn't special to him in the way we all want to be seen as special — as that unique jewel in the crown.

I came to think it was my personality that appealed. We liked to kid around and were comfortable together. I also came to learn that Laura was an emotional volcano whose unpredictable eruptions were a feature, not a bug. Marc needed companionship...and sex...without complications. That was my style as well. So, hand...meet glove.

Some might think I was a wimp for not insisting on more closeness and a greater degree of togetherness, but the truth was I didn't need it, and he absolutely didn't want it, except on his terms. And, since his terms meshed nicely with my needs, we both got what we wanted. I was what he wanted in a partner, someone who was as comfortable as an old shoe, and one that didn't need frequent trips to the cobbler, although now that I think about it, when was the last time you actually went to a cobbler? A more contemporary metaphor might be that I was like an operating system that didn't crash or need constant updating.

One place we were very comfortable was in the bedroom, or in our case, bedrooms. After the first few explosive months, the sex was good but pretty much limited to weekends. While working, I needed to get in a solid eight hours of sleep, so I would get up around five-thirty in order to get to the station, make the 7:08 train, and then get to the courthouse by eight. That meant a nine-thirty bedtime, and even though Marc was also an early riser, he liked to stay up later than me.

So "It" usually happened on Saturday mornings when one of us would crawl into the other's bed, after which Marc would head off to one of the local farmers markets for some fresh produce, then pick up some pastries for a late-morning breakfast — a normal indulgence *pour moi,* but for him, it was a once-a-week deviation from his normal healthy diet. Then, if it was not his weekend with the kids, we might go on a hike or a bike ride followed by dinner out, mostly to restaurants where I wouldn't run into anyone who knew me, which wasn't all that difficult.

I managed to keep Marc a secret for several months. In part, because there was no way I wanted to capitalize on our relationship to find a job, but also because I was afraid I would suddenly have more newly-minted friends than I wanted.

I conducted an internal debate about whom to tell and how much to tell them. I oped for less is more. When I was with friends, I was vague about who I was living with and stuck to the shorthand scripts of "he's in tech," and "we live in Palo Alto."

I purposefully didn't divulge too much because I wasn't sure our relationship would last, and if it was out there in public, I might later have a lot of 'splaining' to do that I didn't want to have to do. Why? I think at base I was as secretive and private as Marc. I did confide all with Lizzie, but made her promise not to tell anyone in our mutual circle of friends and acquaintances anything other than "Cynthia has moved in with someone." Lizzie was that rare person I knew who could keep a secret.

The whole secrecy thing began to fall apart one Saturday morning at the downtown farmer's market when we ran into two of my old law school professors who clearly knew who Marc was. We chatted away pleasantly for a few minutes, and even though they were as mathematically-challenged as most law profs, they were able to put two and two together, so I knew at some point the news would seep out and I would have to think about how I would deal with my being out there as Marc Gordon's live-in girlfriend. (BTW, the fact that the converse was also true in that Marc was living with me was not likely to occur to very many people.)

By the end of the following week I began getting emails from law school friends, the gist of which could pretty much be summed up by, "Hey! What the f...? I hear you're dating Marc Gordon."

The final shoe dropped when word began to seep out to the public-at-large *via* Facebook and Twitter. Although there were no National Enquirer-type headlines like, "Who Is That Mystery Woman With Marc Gordon?" there were a growing number of posts like the one with a pic of us sharing breakfast scones at the Mayfield Cafe. It was hardly the work of a professional *paparazzo*, but rather that of some wonky geek with a cellphone and a likely man-crush on Marc. It had taken a while, but I'd finally been doxxed. One outcome of my very small taste of celebrity was that I began to dress more carefully when we were out in public.

By late May and with the word now out locally, I thought it was time to tell my mom and my sister, as I didn't want them to find out about it second-hand. I called my Mom first and, given her poor experience with men and relationships, all she cared about was that I wouldn't get hurt, which was hardly a ringing endorsement of my ability to handle a relationship. Of course I couldn't promise that I wouldn't, but at this point, our relationship didn't represent a major or long-term commitment on the part of either of us. As for my sister, I knew she would go crazy and she didn't disappoint. A romantic through and through, to her, this was the Cinderella story writ large. She had tons of questions, about Marc, how we met, etc., etc., and ended up asking if I loved him and if he loved me. I told her I didn't think in those terms, and believe it or not, I don't, so I just told her we were comfortable together. She had a hard time processing that as she was a head-over-heels type when it came to romance.

For the past few months, Marc had been having the guest house remodeled, so I told her that when it was finished, she should come up for a visit. I knew when we hung up she would immediately start making plans and that our friends and family communication network, small though it was, would instantly be set ablaze with the news.

So, "the news" gradually became known to my small circle of friends and to his even smaller circle. Eventually it leaked out to a much larger group of people who weren't friends, but who had vested interests. I started getting calls from the development offices of my undergraduate college as well as from the law school. I'd clearly been upgraded and had made it onto the list of those who required the personal touch rather than the standard snail-mail and email solicitations. I had become "a person of substance" simply because of my relationship with Marc, who was an actual "person of substance" — one with a net worth of somewhere between eight and twelve billion dollars, depending on how the markets were doing on a particular day. Nine or ten zeros strung together after a whole number in a financial statement tended to get one all kinds of attention.

After we were out of the "couple closet," so to speak, we tried going out to dinner a few times with some of my friends, but it was awkward. First of all, they were younger and although they tried not to show it, they were definitely intimidated by Marc, so the conversations were often a bit labored, shall we say. Second, they were lawyers interested in law and politics, while Marc was interested in math, physics and techie stuff. It wasn't quite oil and water, but it was close.

It was nice that he pretended to have a good time, but it was apparent to me he basically wasn't interested. I told him that from time to time I needed to get together with my friends, and of course he was okay with that. I know it sounds really strange to say it, but it was clear to me that these were the terms and I could adjust — or not. I was fairly certain this was one of the reasons, if not the main reason for his divorce from Laura, who definitely needed a more active, that is to say "normal," social life with friends, dinners, parties, etc., which she had insisted he be a part of. Obviously, that didn't work out.

Although I didn't flaunt it, by early summer I'd stopped trying to hide it. I just copped to it when asked. "Yes, Marc and I were an item," as they say.

But with me being who I was, I didn't discuss our relationship with anyone other than Lizzie. I could tell that everyone was interested in what was it like to be with someone who, in certain circles, was famous...and rich. Especially the rich part. So, in a way, I felt I was living in a rarified bubble, and I didn't feel comfortable talking about what it was like with those on the outside. I didn't feel special, or different, it was just that everyone's interest felt a little voyeuristic. Not that we were tabloid material, but gossip is gossip. Even in Silicon Valley.

During our first months together, the "what did he see in me?" question was always lurking in the back of my mind. Other than being foodies and exercise nuts, we had few interests in common. But, on the other hand, there were only a few people in the world who truly shared Marc's interests, and fortunately, *pour moi*, as far as I could tell, none were women.

I came to believe the main reason was that I had my own life and made few, if any, demands on him, particularly on his time and attention. For him, our relationship was almost more of a business relationship than a personal one, which, I had to admit, was not entirely comforting in terms of the old self-esteem. He needed to live without distractions in his own interior world. In that way I was a good match for him. And he for me. Not ideal, but good enough for government work.

The question I had to ask myself was, in the long run, would this be "good enough" for me? I wasn't sure. One major sticking point was kids. He had two, and two were enough as far as he was concerned. I was straight with him when I told him I was pretty sure I'd want kids at some point. I would hold off for now, but I couldn't make any long-term promises. Marc was very transactional, and I think he appreciated that I was up front with him about the kids issue. It might seem to some that this was the kind of discussion one would and should have early on with a potential spouse, but we were a long way from being at that point in our relationship. Who knew if it would last past June?

In which case, it would be a personal best for me.

CHAPTER EIGHT

Living With Eccentricity

"What was Marc like?" That was the one question everyone asked. Not that it wasn't worthy of being asked, but most conversations with friends about a new relationship would have started with them asking about *moi*. How was I doing?

Well, okay. I got it, but it did grate. It made me feel like the kid who's always picked last to play right field. However, gentle reader, I won't pretend that question isn't on your mind as well. Soooo...let's dive in, and for the moment I'll keep my thoughts and feelings about our relationship at arm's length and focus on the subject on everyone's mind — Marc Gordon.

I could start by tossing out a long list of adjectives: complex...moody...driven...brilliant, but adjectives don't really tell the whole story. Perhaps he's best explained by my tossing out a few random stories and anecdotes. Were I a decent writer, that's what I would do. Or at least I realize that's how it should be done. So, here goes...

Let me start with his crazy food preferences. For several weeks straight he'd have a kale, cranberry and walnut salad with poppy seed dressing for breakfast. That would be followed by couple of weeks of Indian food — dal, rice, curried veggies and samosas. Next might be hard-boiled eggs and whole-wheat toast washed down with probiotic beet juice. And quinoa. If Bogie and Ingrid always had Paris, we always had quinoa. Quinoa and tofu. Cold quinoa salad. Quinoa burgers. Sadly *pour moi*, there was always quinoa. Okay, I concede that quinoa is healthy, but it left a weird taste in my mouth which even a couple of minutes of intense brushing could not eliminate. Never, ever would he have standard stuff like Cheerios, Sugar Pops or fried eggs and hash browns. However, once a week he did break down and have a Saturday morning croissant and maybe a coffee, which I came to think was his concession to my relatively unhealthy diet, at least "unhealthy" compared to his. He was even disciplined on his indulgences, whereas I couldn't be left alone with a bag of M and M's. He was probably the one person on Earth who could eat just one potato chip —not that he'd ever actually eaten potato chips. (Maybe as a kid, but I wouldn't know.) Like everything else in his life, he'd analyzed and decided what constituted dietary Best Practices and he stuck with them.

He once told me, "If the Hunzas in Pakistan and the Japanese on Okinawa can live to be a hundred, so can I. Although truth be told, I'm shooting for one-twenty."

'Why would you want to?' I asked.

"Aside from the fact that I'd like to just see what it would be like, there's no point in living if you don't have goals."

I then asked if he'd remember me when he was one-twenty and he said, "All you have to do is put your mind to it, make a few lifestyle changes, and you could get there." He then added, "Of course, you'll already have to have been lucky genetically."

I was comforted by the notion he thought it was possible I

might still be around, shrunken and wrinkled though I certainly would be.

After that conversation, I looked up the Hunzas online and found that goat blood was a dietary staple. Needless to say, I never mentioned that to Marc.

About his dietary idiosyncrasies, and calling them "idiosyncrasies" would be the nice way of putting it; "fanaticisms" would be another, although he did have the occasional moments of slippage, or as I came to call them, "Discipline with Detours." He loved pizzas and high-quality artisanal breads, whose excessive carbs (his opinion) he worked off either at the gym or on his long-distance bike rides.

After we'd been together for a few months, he became obsessed with making pizzas and breads and set about developing his expertise in the pursuit of the perfect pie — and the perfect loaf. He bought a stove that injected steam into the oven for making artisan breads and a gas and wood-fired pizza oven which could heat up to a thousand degrees, which, for safety reasons he had installed outside on the patio. He bought organic double-zero flour from Utah, San Marzano tomatoes from Italy, and found a source for buffalo milk and made his own mozzarella. (That would be milk from some kind of water buffalo instead of the Buffalo Bill-type buffalo which first came to my mind.) Glass jars filled with sourdough starters popped up around the kitchen and bowls of dough fermented and proofed day after day in the refrigerators. There were timers and temperature gauges galore. He compiled a small library of books on pizza and bread-making. For a time he was baking half-a-dozen pizzas or loaves of bread every day. Mamma Mia, did we eat a lot of pizza. Hard too believe, but after a while, even Ashley and Dion got tired of it.

He'd make pizzas for lunch and dinner, sometimes just taking a single bite as a sample and if it didn't measure up, he'd toss them out. Being of a frugal nature, I couldn't stand that kind of waste, so after work I began giving them away to neighbors, friends, or sometimes to people just walking by. When I felt neighbors were starting to avoid me as though I were that crazy gardener with a basket full of giant zucchinis, I started driving around after work and handing them out to homeless guys who had never eaten better. When that got to be too much, I arranged for various shelters to come pick up the leftovers. It was a bit of a pain for them, but their inconvenience was always eased by Marc's go-to — a generous dollop of cash. Everything went smoothly until, this being Palo Alto, some bitter, by-the-rules type figured out that we must be a commercial establishment and complained to the health department. This amounted as a call-to-arms for Marc who regularly blew up over bureaucracies and over-regulation — two of his favorite pet peeves. But before he went medieval on them, the cautious lawyer in me reminded him that his pizza oven had been installed on the patio *sans* permit, so did he really want to make a federal case out of it?

I learned never to ask a question about what he was up to in the kitchen unless I really, really, wanted to know everything about enzyme levels, sugar levels, flour-to-water ratios, protein percentages, two-day vs. three-day fermentation schemes, oven temperatures — you name it. All you had to do was ask. And listen. He tried to be concise and keep it interesting, but unless you were deep into bread and pizza lore, it was like listening to a life insurance salesman wax on about actuarial tables.

I once asked him why he was spending all this effort when he could walk down the street and buy a perfectly-good pizza or loaf of bread at any one of a half dozen places nearby.

He looked puzzled then answered, " 'perfectly-good' means 'okay, but not great.' Anything can be improved. Don't be a settler."

He wasn't talking about being a prairie mom.

Nothing was ever done half-way. Or even ninety-nine percent of the way. With Marc, it was all the way or nothing.

In the first few months of "The Great Baking Obsession," he went to a couple of bakeries at two in the morning after promising the owners he was not there to compete with them, but just to see how they operated, and when a Silicon Valley superstar wants to help you knead your dough, and unless you're the pizzarista version of the Seinfeld Soup Nazi, you let him. However, while he was there I think he stole some starter because afterwards the taste of his sourdoughs improved significantly.

But the capper to The Great Pizza Adventure came when he decided he wanted to explore pizza-making at its source — *Bella Italia*, allegedly home to the world's best pizza-makers. I had some vacation days coming and decided to tag along. It was Italy, after all, even though it was the middle of the summer and hot as hell. No need to plan your trip six months in advance to get a cheap fare when you could book online and fly private within hours.

So we did.

Marc had put together a list of the pizzerias he wanted to check out, so we drove madly between Naples, Rome, Florence and various small villages scattered up and down The Boot. At each stop Marc hired a tour guide to serve as an interpreter to ask questions of the pizzanistas who found the fanatical *Americano* very amusing.

Upon landing we rented a Ferrari convertible, which got us a bit of extra attention, even in Italy. "When in Rome..." as the saying goes, although I doubt that most Romans were in a position to rent a Ferrari Italia 458 for a week. Personally, all I needed were a pair of oversized sunglasses, a black silk headscarf and a low-cut dress and I could have been Gina Lollobrigida cruising down the Via Veneto. (Well, maybe not the low-cut dress part, as there was no way I could, if you'll pardon the expression, "stack up" favorably with Gina in that department. Only in my dreams.)

Because we couldn't sample pizzas and pastas all the time, in between tastings we'd check out the local cultural sites. Deciding what to see was my job. Marc wasn't much into sight-seeing for sight-seeings sake, but he tolerated it, and was only interested in the top-of-the-line five-star attractions. In Florence we sped through the Uffizi in under an hour. Touring the Duomo took a little longer because he insisted on climbing the four hundred sixty-three steps to the top. (Believe me, I counted them, going up and coming down). He also hated waiting in lines so we paid up — way up — to jump the queue. So we probably did Europe on Five Thousand Dollars a Day. Undoubtedly a lot more if you factor in the Ferrari rental. One of the virtues of having big bucks, or "Marc money," as I came to call it, was that when you ran into a problem, you had a choice: deal with it or buy your way out. Take a wild guess as to which was Marc's go-to.

I did manage to occasionally break away from the road show and sneak into some of the finer shops, of which there were more than a few. And just to stay somewhat connected to reality, what I bought I put on my own credit card.

One advantage of flying private was that you could load up on wines and fly them home. But because the Ferrari didn't have a trunk the size of a Honda Civic, Marc had most of the wines sent ahead to the airport. He was very taken by the countryside around Florence, so we spent one afternoon in Chianti with a real estate specialist and looked at several villas. Marc had a good sense of architectural aesthetics and was interested in buying something, but one question he always asked was about internet service, and based on the answers given, I could tell that we...or I should say "he," wouldn't be buying anything anytime soon as most of the places were just one step above dial-up.

One afternoon after visiting a pizzeria just north of Florence, Marc said he'd seen enough and was ready to head home. "We've got guys in the states who make pizza just as well or better than here." (At this point in his pizza-making career, he didn't include himself in that category, but could have, IMHO.) Personally, however, I was way past the point of thinking that if I never had another slice of pizza in my life, it would be fine with me.

When we got back, Marc continued his maniacal bread and pizza-making into the fall. Then one afternoon he came home and said, "I picked up a loaf of levain from the Mayfield Bakery." It was over.

Stunned, I asked why and he said, "There's no Moore's Law in pizza-making." (Okay, look it up.) "Once you get to a certain level, you're no longer even making incremental improvements, you're just making sure there's no slippage. And when that's all you're doing, it's boring" IMHO, "boring"was the operative term in his statement. Once Marc got to that point with anything, it was *finito*.

Was all this effort and time spent in the pursuit of the perfect pizza something worthy of his talents? That's debatable, of course, but what wasn't in question was that he pursued his passions — with passion.

But let me move on beyond his quirky food preferences. One Saturday morning after we'd been together a couple of months, I'd slept in and Marc texted me saying he wanted to show me something downstairs. (Yep, the house was big enough so that texting was a good way to avoid having to tromp up and down the stairs to communicate.)

I put on a robe, went downstairs and saw that Marc had laid out a row of handguns on the dining room table.

"What's this about?" I asked.

"You need to know how to protect yourself."

"Why? We have security...you know, Carl and his guys."

"Yeah, but they can look the other way. Turn their backs. Fall asleep. Whatever. You never know. And forget about calling the police in an emergency. By the time they show up, all they'll do is put up yellow tape around the crime scene and take pictures of the bodies."

(That was pretty grim, I thought.)

He picked up a revolver with what looked like a foot-long barrel and checked the chamber for bullets. There weren't any.

Lesson number one.

"Remember, a gun is like a parachute. When you really, really, need one and don't have one, chances are you'll never need one again."

I'd grown up in Arizona where there were plenty of guns around, just not in our house. We were solid liberals, so I said, "I just don't feel safe around guns."

"You mean you don't trust yourself around guns?"

"No, it isn't that. Just having them around makes me nervous."

"We've had them around, you just didn't know about it."

"But I do now."

"So are you nervous now?"

I didn't want to go there so I said nothing.

Marc continued, "Look, I feel safer knowing we have them. What I don't feel safe about is knowing the kind of people who are out there. Most people will always do the right thing while two percent or so will take advantage of whatever the circumstances allow, and then there's that small but significant number of psychopaths who would shoot you just to watch you die."

He paused, then asked, "There was a song about that, right?

"Johnny Cash."

He proceeded to show me some of the basics: how to hold a gun, how to stand and how to aim and fire. Of course, this being Palo Alto, we didn't do any actual firing away inside, but after the living-room lesson, he announced we were going to spend the rest of the morning at a shooting range.

Having already had what I thought was a lesson, I asked him what else was there that I needed to know. "Isn't it just ready…aim…fire?"

"It's not like what you see on TV."

After a quick stop at the Mayfield Cafe for our usual Saturday breakfast of croissants, coffee for me and green tea for him, we drove out to a shooting range in the hills behind Sunnyvale. Getting out of the car in the parking lot, I heard what sounded like the Fourth of July on steroids.

On the range I quickly discovered that my hand-eye coordination was pretty darn good — maybe even better than Marc's. Of course, I was only shooting with a .22 pistol and after consistently hitting the target, I was getting a little cocky. Then, just to give me an idea of what it was like with a real gun, Marc slipped a single bullet into a Smith and Wesson .44 Magnum and handed it to me. I was barely able to lift the damned thing, but I took my stance, aimed, and pulled the trigger. The kick from the Dirty Harry Special almost broke my wrist and nearly knocked me on my butt, which Marc and the other guys on the range thought was pretty funny. After receiving my instant-karma lesson in humility, we dropped down to a 9mm Sig Sauer, which had a recoil I could handle.

The upshot of all this was I found I liked pulling the trigger and letting the lead fly, all the while feeling that little tingle of empowerment, if you know what I mean. I did think that if my judge could see me now he'd probably have a heart attack or, at a minimum, can my sorry butt on the spot. Not to mention what my law school profs and fellow students would have thought about it.

As we were packing up, I asked Marc if he would trust me to keep a gun under my pillow.

He smiled and said, "That, I'll have to think about."

On our way home, this pistol-packing mama found herself silently humming country and western songs about honky-tonks, pickup trucks and romances gone sour. No stereotyping there.

One thing Marc and I had in common was working out, although we rarely exercised together. He used the workout room in the basement, but I liked to get out, and my time at the gym pretty much became my social life, if you could call it a life. For me, it was mainly a way of hanging out and doing a little people-watching while keeping in shape. I would sometimes stop off after work for a quick workout before heading home for dinner. (At some nebulous point during the summer, I began to to refer to Marc's place as "home," which I attributed to me feeling more comfortable about our relationship.)

If I was mostly a "weekend warrior" in the exercise department, Marc was a true "fitness fanatic." He worked out in the basement at least an hour a day and a couple of times a week he would take off on an extended bike ride. He had a half-dozen light-weight bikes hanging in the garage and it was a mystery to me what his criterion was for determining which among them would be chosen for a particular ride, but

I knew that asking about it would have led to an hour-long information dump on the minuscule differences between the various models. I did check out a couple of them on line and found each one cost between five and ten thousand bucks. For a bike. Unbelievable to *moi*.

About once a month he would join up on a weekend ride with a group of mostly guys and they would cruise up, down and around the peninsula hills for forty to fifty miles or so. I once asked him with whom he was riding and he mentioned a few names. I did a quick calculation of the combined net worth of this clubby little peloton and it probably approached the GDP of a couple of medium-sized European nations. Hell's Angels, they were not. However, I had to admit that some of those Tour de France wannabes looked pretty good in their tight-fitting lycra outfits.

Despite his semi-retirement there were continual demands on his time: a request to give a speech, teach a class, sit on a board — most of which he managed to avoid. And there were always those asks for charitable donations. He was generous but not foolish with his money, and it soon became clear to me what he valued most was his time. He didn't want to be sucked into something that took away from whatever it was he was thinking about. He freely admitted he was able to find enough ways to waste time on his own without being drawn into someone else's fantasy. (My mind immediately went to his six-month long pizza-making obsession.)

Shortly after I'd moved in, he got an unofficial inquiry about returning to his old company which, though not failing, was treading water. He declined, in part because he didn't want to be seen as pulling a Steve Jobs, but also because, by his own admission, he was not an operations guy. He'd been fired once over his managerial shortcomings and he didn't want a repeat performance of that, especially with a company he'd lost interest in. He maintained that any halfway-competent MBA could run ByteAnalysis, and unless they came up with a great new product, "ByteMe" wasn't going anywhere, and if by some miracle, if he were to go on and create the "next big thing," he certainly wasn't going to share it with the back-stabbers.

Still, I worried about Marc. He was clearly searching for a new mission in life, but thus far hadn't found one, although not for a lack of trying. Occasionally I would find jottings of indecipherable mathematical formulas on papers left out on the kitchen island, and in his office/study he had a giant white board covered with similar scribblings, none of which I remotely understood.

He also spent time in what I came to call "The Black Hole," a completely sound-proofed, light-proofed room he'd had built in the basement. You entered The Hole through two doors separated by a small antechamber, and when you closed the second door behind you, The Hole was completely dark, and by "dark," I mean "totally dark." You can't imagine what "totally dark" is like until you've tried it. Once you were in and your eyes adjusted to it, the only thing you could see were retinal images — the internal light show your brain creates. Marc's theory was that your eyes were the enemy of creativity because it's almost impossible to ignore the continuous stream of images coming in, which your brain then has to process.

The Hole was furnished, so to speak, with a twin bed, a comfortable Lazy-Boy recliner, a desk and a lamp. There was no computer and no refrigerator because, with no other noise, even the soft hum of an electric motor would sound like Niagara Falls. There was an adjoining bathroom with a sink and a toilet, and Marc kept The Hole supplied with spring water, Kind bars, dried fruits and assorted other snackibles so he didn't have to leave and go up to the kitchen when he was hungry.

When he was down there, he wore an Apple watch which could provide enough light to allow him to make his way around or find the door when he needed to, but he always set it to airplane mode so as not to be interrupted.

If I weren't home, he'd text me to let me know when I should go down and extract him because he could easily lose track of time. Once he was down there for ten hours and thought it was two. Once just to see what it was like, I spent an hour down there, at least I think it was an hour because it was hard to tell how long it really was. I fell asleep in the Lazy-Boy and woke up terrified. To me, it was, in a word... creepy, but Marc liked it because it allowed him to think without distractions. A bomb could go off upstairs and you wouldn't hear it in The Hole.

Because we had separate bedrooms and kept slightly-different hours, I wasn't always aware of where he was and what he was up to. Occasionally he would disappear in the middle of the night, and it would be obvious to even the dimmest among us to think he might be seeing someone else. After fretting about it for a while, I finally managed to bring it up one morning in a non-threatening way, so instead of asking "Where were you last night?" I phrased it as, "I heard you drive out last night. Is everything okay?"

He told me he liked to take long drives in the middle of the night when there was hardly any traffic. He would head up Page Mill Road to Skyline Boulevard or just drive up and down the nearly-deserted 280 freeway in the foothills. He said the rhythm of driving stimulated his thinking and sometimes gave him new ideas. He'd hired a driver a couple of times, but found it distracting to even be aware of someone else's driving rhythms, and once he even fell asleep riding in the back seat, thus defeating the purpose of his peculiar midnight ramble. After telling me about it, I volunteered and drove one Saturday night, thinking in my womanly way that it would be a good chance for us to spend some quality time together, but he sat in the back for the entire ride, saying nothing — as was the plan. Why I thought it might be different, I don't know.

By now you've probably gotten the picture that life with Marc was not filled with exciting travel adventures (the Italy trip being the exception), symphony galas, opening night at the opera or the other traditional social events attended by those with more money than sense. Quite the opposite: we were homebodies.

Our social life, so-called, was almost non-existent. Marc had only a few friends he cared to see, and of course, that "social life," if one could call it that, was totally-related to all things techie. Working on high-end math problems and computer science issues evenings, nights and weekends was something that interested only a relative few, but those who did were his best-buds.

As for me, I would occasionally invite Lizzie over for a Saturday afternoon "dip and dish," wherein we just sat by the pool and talked. Although I had other friends, I felt uncomfortable having them over because it felt like I was showing off. Instead, I'd meet them somewhere else for lunch or the occasional dinner.

At first, we tried having a few friends over, but after a couple of mini-disasters, that was definitely a no-go, mainly as we had no friends in common, one of us would inevitably be the odd person out. Not that Marc actually had that many friends he wanted to have over for dinner. And of those he did have, well…they leaned heavily towards the geeky end of the evolutionary spectrum, and what most people would see as normal socializing was of as little interest to them as it was to Marc. And food-wise, they hadn't progressed much beyond the traditional techie diet of Cokes and pizza, although during Marc's obsessive pizza-making phase, they would do a double-take after tasting one of his creations and say with surprise, "This is pretty f…king good," or, "You really made this?" Not the cardboard-crust pizzas they were used to getting from…well, I don't want to get sued here, so fill in that blank on your own.

So, dinner with friends was a total waste of time for him. When traditional events such as Thanksgiving, Christmas or his kids' birthdays arrived that called for a social interaction, he was okay with them as long as he could disappear if he needed to. His motto was "thoughts are fleeting." He believed that when you got an idea, you needed to immediately go where it took you or you could lose it forever. Granted, he understood that most of these ideas went nowhere, but you didn't know that when the idea first hit, so you had to go with it because it could be the one you'd been waiting for.

It was clear that being creative in his internal world was what he lived for — his "work," if you will. Could I handle all the idiosyncrasies that came with Life With Marc? Yes, I could, or at least I could at that particular point in time.

CHAPTER NINE

My Brilliant Career

But, back to *moi*. In mid-June an overhead water pipe burst in the judge's chambers directly over our clerks' cubbyhole. While the ceiling was being repaired, The Three Amigos were forced to move out of our water-soaked cubicles into quarters even more cramped. After a couple of days of suffering from too much togetherness, our judge, in a rare show of mercy, declared that only one of us needed to show up in person during the month or so it would take to repair the damage. So the two junior clerks, now officially-deemed less-essential, were allowed to work from home for the duration. Break my heart. Were I to get really lucky, I might never have to go back to work in the courthouse before my clerkship was up at the end of August.

Before *le deluge* I'd been using my personal laptop for those times when I'd work from home, but now, because the situation was semi-permanent, my little old underpowered laptop didn't cut it with Marc. He set up an elaborate computer system in one of the many spare rooms in the Palo Alto Palace, as I had started to call it. He, or "we," as I could now say, had a super high-speed internet connection that would have been the envy of the IT department at most colleges. I didn't dare tell him that my internet needs did not require the ten gazillion bps connection he'd set me up with, because I considered what he'd done to be, if not a "show of love," at least a "show of affection," and was pretty much the main kind of emotional expression he was capable of.

One of the plusses of this new arrangement was that working from home allowed me to see how he spent his average day. He had a routine: early workout or bike ride, breakfast, computer time, think time, a quick pit stop in the kitchen for a salad and sandwich or maybe lunch downtown, more think time, a grocery run to either Trader Joe's or Whole Foods, then dinner, then bed. And except for the lengthy but temporary detour of obsessive pizza-making, it rarely varied.

Once in a while and usually late in the afternoon because Marc discouraged earlier visits, a random dude would drop by and they'd sit by the pool or in front of Marc's computers and yack away. From the bits of conversation I was able to overhear, there was very little typical guy-talk, unless discussions of computer operations or esoteric mathematical formulas were typical.

Before I began working from home, I would occasionally came back from the courthouse to find a Lamborghini, a Ferrari or some other fancy car parked in the driveway. The first time it happened, I thought, okay, he finally caved and bought into the stereotype; but as it turned out, the car wasn't Marc's, but instead a thought-to-be babe-magnet owned by one of his geeky friends. However, I came home one time to find a perfectly-detailed vintage Aston-Martin convertible parked out front and had hopes that some version of Sean Connery's James Bond had come a-visiting, but no such luck; instead, it was just another one of his nerdy buds, but admittedly one with taste. I was sometimes tempted to leave my banged-up Toyota parked up tight on the driver's side just to watch his friends freak out and check for door-dings, but this remained a thought-crime only. I'm just tossing that in here to let you know I was not always Ms. Sweetness and Light.

But, as usual, I digress. Enough anecdotes about the weirdness of Life With Marc. Back to the story.

By the start of the summer I was getting seriously worried about what to do after my clerkship ended. The sad truth was I'd been dilly-dallying. I'd long since given up on the DC offer, but had nothing in mind to take its place and I did have my law school debt to consider. It had been deferred while I was clerking, but unless my next job was with a non-profit or in public service, I'd have to start paying it down. My loan was in the low six-figures, so it was fairly-substantial. If it weren't for Marc, I most likely would have taken a job with a firm in New York or D.C. where I'd be making enough to start paying it off, but obviously that was not something I now wanted to do. And even if I were to take something with a local firm, I'd be expected to throw myself into it if not 24/7, at least 12/6 with an occasional Sunday off, if I were lucky. And ditto for going the non-profit route, as even it would require a nearly-similar time commitment but for less money, so I'd just be postponing the inevitable.

A few months earlier when I was considering various options, I met with one of the associate deans at Stanford to see if there were any legal research positions for which I might be considered. These were often part-time, which would have been ideal, and were usually set aside for women, who, for family reasons, didn't want to commit to the soul-crushing hours most lawyers worked. At the time, I hadn't been "outed," so I purposely didn't divulge why I didn't want a full-time job, but there was obviously only one reason — Marc Gordon.

We met and the dean was non-committal, in part because

he was taking a sabbatical starting in the fall, so anything he had was on hold, but also because he was skeptical of my motivation or rather, my apparent lack of motivation in getting serious about my career.

He hadn't gotten to his position without having some insight, so he began to probe as to why I wasn't charging ahead on the more traditional career paths and warned me that getting sidetracked so soon after leaving law school was not a good thing. I didn't tell him I needed to stay in Palo Alto for personal reasons, but I'm pretty sure he figured it was something like that. In the end, he advised me to check in with Career Services and see if I could line something up through them. He wished me luck and said he'd let me know if anything came up before he went on sabbatical. Given his overall lack of enthusiasm, I took that as not even a "definite maybe," especially considering it was little to no-experience *moi* who would be resting at the bottom of his resumé pile.

Even discounting the Marc factor, the bigger issue was that I was still undecided about a permanent career direction, now that I'd figured out patent law wasn't for me (nor was I for it, BTW.) However, as the dean had said, I needed to keep moving forward to make sure I didn't have a career face-plant, although I'm sure some would say I'd already dithered long enough so that a full-frontal face-plant was definitely in play.

But now that I was "working from home," and we all know what that means, I was able to spend a fair amount of time trolling for jobs online. I contacted some of my law school buds asking for leads and advice, although what I got was plenty of advice and few leads, none of which had led anywhere.

I even spent some time down in The Hole. But unfortunately, it didn't work for me, although on these occasions it proved to be a nice place for a nap, from which I awoke refreshed but unenlightened. No Eureka moment *pour moi.*

By midsummer I was beginning to feel a bit desperate, but I realized I didn't have to make the huge monthly nut most law grads needed to pay the rent, their student loans, their car payments, gym memberships, etc., etc. I had a built-in cushion named Marc to fall back on, not that I would ever have asked him for actual cash. And even though we were not exactly living like the Kardashians, life at the Palo Alto Palace was pretty sweet. However, I felt conflicted by this because there was no way I could ever pay anything close to my "fair share" of our expenses. But there was another issue: I was determined to keep working, not just from a financial point of view, which was on-its-face ridiculous because of Marc's wealth, but from the point of view of personal integrity. I did not want to be or be seen as a gold-digging *arriviste*, or worse, seen as one who was not just a semi-independent girlfriend, but a kept woman. I had my self-respect and I wanted to keep it. I figured I could maintain my respectability if I could somehow bring in roughly what I'd been making as a clerk. At that point in my life, I wasn't setting up a forty-year retirement plan, but was rolling the dice to just get by for the next few months to see what developed with Marc.

Just before we'd jetted off to Italy, one of my law school friends told me about an on-line company that farmed out legal work on a per-job basis. I hoped it wouldn't come to that, but I knew that I needed to have something of my own to hang my hat on. So, when we got back from Italy, I began to get serious about my next career move. I'd always been one who liked to have all the I's dotted and T's crossed before moving ahead, and although I admired those who could blindly leap into the great unknown, totally-confident in their ability to overcome whatever obstacles stood in their way —

that wasn't me.

But, after several weeks of agonizing deep-think, I did the unexpected. I took that leap; although admittedly it was a very small leap off a very low ledge. I decided I would strike out on my own and give it a go as a real-life, jack-of-all-trades attorney — one with an office with my name on the door.

I'd taken some mediation classes in law school, liked them, and found I just needed to take a few online courses to get certified. I figured I'd specialize in mediation and negotiation, but I obviously would take anything that came through the door, under the door or over the transom, assuming there were still offices with transoms, which I believe have something to do with air circulation.

There were tough decisions to be made right out of the gate: should the name on the door be "Cynthia Burrows - Attorney at Law," or should I hang out a shingle that read, "The Law Offices of Cynthia Burrows?" Marc suggested "Cynthia Burrows, Mouthpiece for the Mob," which undoubtedly would have paid better than any work I was likely to get, but I was pretty sure hit men and mobsters were in short supply in Palo Alto.

One thing I was certain of was that I did not want to work from home, even though the "home" in question was nearly as spacious as Windsor Castle and undoubtedly more comfortable. But aside from not wanting to get in Mark's way, I felt the need to have a connection with normal, everyday life, something I hoped an office would give me. It was something my temporary exile from the courthouse while our cubicles were being repaired had convinced me of. So I signed the lease for a relatively inexpensive office in downtown Palo Alto not far from the railroad station. Also not far from Whole Foods, which was a plus. It was on the second floor and had a small waiting room right off the hallway, which eventually could serve as a space for my future receptionist, guy or gal Friday, legal assistant... whatever. It even had a view of an all-day parking lot. Such a deal.

After my clerkship ended (no going-away party, BTW), Marc and I spent Labor Day weekend getting my new digs ready. We assembled some Ikea furniture without a major conflict and filled a bookshelf with a couple of rows of fake law books, which I hoped would give the place a veneer of professionalism. Marc set up my computer system and donated a mini-fridge and a Keurig to the cause. A couple of potted plants, a few tasteful prints and the place would be mine. I also reminded myself to get my law school diploma framed. Now all I needed were clients.

I opened up right after Labor Day and waited for business to pour in, but, of course, it didn't. I knew it wouldn't, but one could always hope. The sad truth was clients were going to be hard to come by and there was no way there'd be any walk-in business. Plus the rent for this dumpster of an office was more than for my old apartment in Mountain View. I didn't like to think about it, but I couldn't have swung this if I weren't living with Marc. On the other hand, if I weren't living with Marc I would have found a real job, so I was determined to make this work.

I spent most of my time calling and emailing law school friends, non-law school friends as well as people I barely knew, letting them know I had started my own practice and if they could kick anything my way, it would be deeply-appreciated. I placed ads in business and law publications, the local newspapers and on-line venues, although as a "professional," there were limits as to how much and what kind of advertising I could do. And because I still had some standards, I refrained from plastering my mug onto a freeway billboard.

As it turned out, my first client was Marc.

He'd been haggling with various city departments and agencies over the guest house remodel which had taken much longer than he'd wanted or expected. In his opinion, the primary area of expertise of the planning department bureaucrats was foot-dragging. Marc and I had already had some lengthy conversations about the problem and I could tell that he was fed up. So, one day he called and made an appointment to meet me at my office, which I thought was hardly necessary as we could have discussed it at home, but he insisted. So we met and basically he turned the whole mess over to me and offered to pay me to take care of it. Considering that I was living at his house rent-free, I would have done it *pro bono*, but he was adamant and I knew there was no point in arguing. Besides, there was no getting around the fact that I could use the money, if only to bolster my self-esteem.

So I took over, dove into the issues and after several weeks of nudging, prodding, cajoling and threatening, got the permits, approvals and inspection sign-offs necessary to nudge the remodel closer to the finish line. As for me, I got a real-life lesson in dealing with bureaucracies as well as a nice check, which allowed me to maintain the illusion that I was a successful, real-life attorney.

But if just handling a client's case successfully wasn't enough, I had another incentive for getting the guest house ready. I wanted to have people stay with us and Marc didn't. At the moment, the state of play was "no guests," even for an overnight. However, the reality was that when the guest house was finished, it wouldn't be for guests, but would be the place where Marc could hang out or hide out when we actually had guests. He wasn't against having company *per se*, it was just that he couldn't know whether or not he'd want to be around when they were. He'd made it clear that just by being living, breathing human beings with living, breathing human being wants and needs, guest were a distraction. Were he in the mood to socialize, fine, but if he wasn't, he wouldn't — and he didn't want anyone around. But even he realized that wasn't practical, so the guest house would be a place of refuge where he could hole up until the guests removed themselves.

A people-person he was not.

But just as the guest house redo was nearing completion, a late November phone call sent the renovation into overdrive, and our Christmas plans went from complicated to chaotic.

CHAPTER TEN

The Duchess of Dallas

We had planned to escape to Utah right after Christmas for a week of skiing with Ashley, Dion and one of the nannies, but then Marc's parents, or more precisely, Marc's mom, decided she just had to see her grandkids. At Christmas. Granted, what with the divorce and all, it had been a while. They'd spent the previous Christmas on the East Coast with Marc's brother's and sister's families, and this year she decreed it was our turn. Or again more precisely, Marc's turn. He was not thrilled. Based on past experience, he was dreading it, and as the one most likely to be the odd-person-out, so was I.

They, of course, would be staying with us, although when his mom called, she proclaimed, "We'll stay in a hotel if we have to," which was something Marc had to mull over because his first response was not, "No way you're staying in a hotel, you're staying with us!" A dutiful son he was not, but in the end he caved.

I thought about ducking out on the fun and heading to Arizona just to get out of the way, but when I brought this up, Marc uncharacteristically blew up and insisted I stay. I didn't think it was really a fair ask, but when he blurted out that he needed me to be here with him, how could I not? This was not the sort of admission he'd ever made before, so I decided I would take one for the team.

As a result, I skipped going to AZ for any part of the holidays and promised my mom and my sister they were welcome to pop up for a visit sometime early next year, now that the guest house was certain to be finished.

Because he was definitely not the type for serious personal introspection, Marc had never really talked much about his family. In his opinion, dwelling on the past got in the way of getting on with life, but with this surprise visit, the floodgates opened and it all poured out.

Marc's parents had met in Austin when his dad was a grad student studying petroleum engineering. His mom was getting a degree in elementary education, but she never taught, thank god, thus saving a couple of generations of young Texans from permanent psychological damage. It turned out his dad was highly-skilled at finding "awl," as they say in Texas, and as an independent contractor who got a royalty for each new find, the family moved around a lot. By never spending more than three years in one place, the kids were like military brats in their rootlessness, completing tours of duty in Saudi Arabia, The Emirates, Alberta, North Dakota and finally Midland, Texas, where Marc went to high school. As a newbie and a nerd, Marc didn't fit in with the popular crowd, not that he wanted to. However, he did start a computer club and wrote a program for a video game which he sold to Electronic Arts for enough money to have paid for a couple of years of college, but his dad made enough that he didn't have to. While at Midland High, he tried to abolish the student government, thinking it a complete waste of time as a powerless rubber stamp. His move failed, of course. He was easily the class valedictorian but refused to give a speech saying, "No one wants to hear what I really think." When he left for MIT, his mom declared there would be no more moving around. She was tired of living in the boonies and declared she and Marc's younger sister were living either in Dallas or Houston and Marc's dad could commute from there to wherever. They settled on Dallas and had been there for almost fifteen years, by far the longest stint of their marriage.

Marc was a middle child. His older brother lived in Scarsdale and was a partner at one of the major NY law firms. He was full of himself and he and Marc didn't get along. Despite his own success, he was jealous of Marc's and belittled him for losing control of ByteAnalysis. He was also envious of Marc's net worth, but short of rewriting the will and murdering his brother, there was no way he was ever going to have that kind of dough.

According to Marc, his younger sister was a sweetheart, although they rarely saw each other as she was wrapped up in her own life. While in grad school at the University of Texas, she'd married a fellow psychology student and was now busy raising their two young kids while her husband began his teaching career as an assistant prof at a college just outside Washington, D.C. — a place Marc hated in the abstract as well as in the concrete, and consequently never wanted to visit.

His mom was a woman with strong opinions: often wrong but never in doubt. Surprisingly, the Mom and Laura got along well, which may have been a case of "like meeting like." According to Marc, his dad had equally-strong opinions but wisely chose to keep them to himself, mainly as a way of avoiding domestic conflict. On this visit, he would simply be along for the ride.

With their arrival expected a week before Christmas,

massive back-and-forth negotiations took place between the House of Laura and the House of Marc, which were interspersed with strategic planning sessions between Marc and me. We agreed the first order of business was to get them out from under us as much as possible. Marc hoped the grandparents would take the kids down to Carmel for two or three of days, along with a nanny, of course. Then up to to SF to see Santa and the Christmas lights on Union Square. For that, he would hire one of Carl's guys to play tour guide so he wouldn't have to go.

Then everyone would come over for Christmas Eve and Christmas Day festivities. Because the parental unit was from Texas, some type of seared meat was expected to be the main attraction at dinner. Although not a full-on vegetarian, Marc balked at the idea of cooking a turkey or roasting some kind of beast in his kitchen, so…thank god for Whole Foods. Laura would host Christmas breakfast and the present-opening carnage, *sans* her trumpet-playing BF, who wisely chose to spend the day with his friends, family, or whatever — anywhere but here. I was envious.

When this all started after Thanksgiving, Marc pushed hard on the contractors to get the guest house ready in time. Complaints about working nights and weekends were resolved in the usual Marc manner with large infusions of cash.

While all this was going on, I realized at some point I'd never seen any family pictures around the house. Maybe they lived in a drawer somewhere, but none were out on display. At first I thought it was just one more thing Marc was secretive about, but when his mom arrived like a Texas tornado taking dead aim at a trailer park, I understood.

The first words out of her mouth when she walked into the house was to announce that they weren't staying in the guest house. "We came here to spend time with you and the kids and not be locked away in some cottage." It was not a request.

Tall and platinum blonde with finely-chiseled features, she was probably too hoity-toity to have been Miss Texas in her younger days, but easily could have been. You know the type: the kind of person who wears pearls to breakfast or dresses up to head down to the Seven-Eleven, not that she'd ever actually set foot in a Seven-Eleven. She fit no one's image of a granny.

Marc's dad was a lanky, taciturn good-old-boy. He wore one of those Bolo string ties with a turquoise clasp along with a matching belt to hold up his jeans. All that was missing from the look was a pair of cowboy boots, which he later told me were too uncomfortable to wear on the plane or around the house. If his wife was from Nieman-Marcus, he was from the Stetson-wearing Gary Cooper camp. Strong and silent. By and large he ignored his wife's bluster and like Marc, inhabited his own universe, although he seemed more content living in his world than my guy was in his.

Marc's mom was a non-stop talking machine and after greeting Marc with a perfunctory hug, she commandeered the transfer of luggage from the limo to the the foyer and then began a tour of the house to select the room they'd be staying in. On her way to the second floor, she brushed by me in a way that presumed I was one of the nannies. Marc managed to stop her and introduced us and it was clear he'd never mentioned me to her. She sized me up from head to toe and extended her hand in a manner that suggested I could either shake it or bend over and give it a kiss as though she were the Queen of the Kingdom of Texas. I chose to shake rather than bend a knee. Marc's dad was more accommodating and we had a brief chat while his wife led Marc upstairs for the bedroom selection.

"Welcome to the family," he said quietly.

And so it began.

Almost none of our carefully-laid plans went off as scheduled. Dion came down with the sniffles so we had to scuttle the three-day trip to Carmel. Various day trips took its place, including one to the Exploratorium in San Francisco, which was followed by a walk out onto the Golden Gate Bridge where we were practically alone because only crazy people would take such a walk in December when the wind cut through several layers of North Face fleece like, well…it was pretty darn cold. The Duchess of Dallas wisely stayed in the van with Dion after saying, "If you freeze to death out there, don't say I didn't warn you." For once I had to agree with her, but I freely chose freezing to death over spending time sitting in the van with her.

This was followed two days later with another visit to San Francisco to see Santa and the Christmas lights on Union Square. And because five-year-old Dion was still a Believer in the Claus, older sister Ashley, clear-eyed realist that she was, was kind enough to not spoil his fun.

When we weren't out on a day trip, Laura and Marc's mom spent time at the Stanford Shopping Center, and thank God for favors large and small (and this was one of the large variety), I was left out of that particular loop. One day Marc's dad decamped to Stanford to talk shop over lunch with a couple of petroleum engineering profs. Even though he was not an academic, they gave him all the respect he deserved as an oil-finding god. When not a tag-along on one of the day trips, he would settle into a chair in the late afternoon and read the Wall Street Journal, accompanied by a tumbler of Jack Daniels. No ice.

Although we were heavily dependent on Whole Foods and various catering services, there was plenty of food prep, table-setting and cleanup to be done, especially with dietary needs ranging from T-bone steaks to quinoa burgers. Because it was an all-hands-on-deck moment, I was permitted to do some slicing and dicing in the kitchen, something Marc usually didn't allow, and even Henrietta was dragooned into assisting, although she was adamant about having Christmas off, and so strong was her insistence that Marc didn't even attempt to bribe her.

With most of their dietary restrictions lifted for the occasion, the grandkids had a field day. Although the parents tried to hold the line, every excursion seemed to end with the kids scarfing-down some kind of high-calorie treat. Some might say that's what grandparents are for: creating chaos and then walking away. Marc's Mom was very good at the chaos part.

I wasn't dismissed, exactly, but after five days of showing not the slightest interest in me, I doubted the Duchess even knew my last name. The kids didn't exactly take to her either as she was not the kindly old grandmother they'd imagined, but they were good soldiers. Near the end of the visit, Dion asked, "When are we going skiing?" in a tone that suggested his real question was, "When is grandma leaving?" although perhaps I was just projecting.

Even though I had never been the life of the party in high school, I hadn't been a wallflower, but I was grateful to play one during this visit. One night after everyone had gone to bed, I did have a nice chat with Marc's dad as we sat in front of the fire and drank some Kentucky bourbon, straight up. I did not regret the conversation, but as a novice whiskeyphile, I paid the price the next morning.

The opposite of his whirlwind wife, Marc's dad had stories aplenty about life in the oil patch, which, at his level, did not involve fights outside of honky-tonks, but were more about high-level graft and corruption involving Saudi princes (no princesses, of course) and Russki wheeler-dealers who were much more menacing and life-threatening than any Texas roughneck.

All of this led up to the dual, or perhaps "dueling," grand finales, Christmas Eve and Christmas Day.

Laura's parents drove down from Sacramento so they had the kids at Laura's for Christmas Eve. Then, with all grandparents in attendance, there would a joint present-opening at Laura's on Christmas morning, after which we would host everyone for a Christmas Day dinner, the grandparents' last hurrah before heading back to Texas.

Christmas morning was tough *pour moi*. Marc and his parents headed down to Laura's for the present-opening frenzy, which left me alone for a few hours. I realized that on days like this I would always be sharing him with Laura. I felt we were at a point in our relationship where I could have tagged along, but the truth was I was relieved to be out of the presence of the Duchess for a few hours, especially since I still had the rest of Christmas Day to deal with. So I made the best use of my reprieve by calling my mom and sister and, for the moment, avoided becoming collateral damage.

So Christmas came and went and we survived. The next day, when Marc returned after dropping them off at the airport, he came upstairs, threw himself on the bed and said, "I never...ever...want to do that again." Were this a legal proceeding, I would immediately have filed a concurring opinion.

The good news was that we were now free and would be leaving soon for that week of skiing in Utah.

So, two days later we were in Park City. We had the kids and one of the nannies for the week and surprisingly, there'd been no tug-of-war with Laura about that, especially considering how big she was on celebrating all-things

Christmas, including the fact that she'd had to share the kids with us during the grandparents' visit. She was off to Cabo and was unusually-vague about the unnamed friends she was going with. Adding to the circumstantial evidence that funny business might be happening was the fact that the trumpet-playing, motorcycle-riding boyfriend wouldn't be joining her, as he was performing non-stop with the symphony through the holidays. Call me skeptical about the what she was up to, but…none of my business.

We rented what some in the billionaire's club might have considered a modest place on a hillside above Park City for only thirty thousand for the week, which worked out to about a dollar per square foot. I'm exaggerating, of course, but it seemed like all of us could have slept in a different room every night and not have hit them all. It was amazing what I'd become accustomed to. Marc now depended on me for handling car-rentals, mansion rentals and even for arranging the private jet rentals. Detail-minded as he was, he was good at it, but it also distracted him from his so-called "mission in life" (my words, not his), as he would never say something so egocentric, even if true. The fact that he trusted me to do all that was nice, but I also felt somewhat taken advantage of as one whose time was seen as less valuable.

Coming from the sun-drenched part of Arizona, skiing was new to me, but I discovered I had a fairly-good intuitive sense about how to get down the average slope without breaking anything. I held my own with the kids who were already decent skiers, having been on several trips before — but of course without *moi*. Marc was good at skiing as he was at most everything.

What I loved about skiing was not so much the getting down the hill part, but being able to stand at the top of the mountain and "listen," if that's the right term, to the nearly-absolute silence, which was in total contrast to the week-long ringing in my ears of a voice I'd rather never hear again. We all needed this R & R: the kids, the nanny, but especially Marc and me.

CHAPTER ELEVEN

Course Correction

Après le deluge of the holidays and the invasion of the parental unit, it was a relief to get back to our normal, everyday, boring routine. By February, we'd been living together for a year and it had been four since Marc had been forced out of his company. He was still staying busy working on whatever it was he was working on, although exactly what he was up to was a mystery to me and to most everyone else.

Every couple of weeks he would spend an afternoon at a venture capital shop on Sand Hill Road and sit in on pitch sessions for startups. If he was interested, he would follow up to get more detail, but he always made it clear he did not want to get involved in the day-to-day operations of any new enterprises. He once confessed to me that his greatest failure at ByteAnalysis was that he was a lousy manager. Like a lot of tech whizzes, he thought running a business was easy and had little respect for the MBA types who did, but early on in his reign as CEO and definitely after his ouster, he realized it wasn't as simple as it looked. Plus, as an idea guy, he saw managing people and running an organization as major-league time-sucks.

As for me, I was doing okay as a solo practitioner, but I couldn't say my business, and it was a "business," was going gangbusters. After Marc got me started as client *numero uno*, I managed to pick up a couple of mediations as well as several contract jobs sent my way by my law school buds. All in all, it was just enough to allow me to maintain the illusion that the practice was viable. When I started out, I figured I'd give it a year and then reassess; however, even after just a few months, I realized flying solo was not what I wanted to be doing, which led me back to the same-old, same-old...the relationship dilemma. If one looked at it objectively, I was, like Pluto, a minor planet at the far edge of the solar system revolving around Marc's sun. And even though he was also at a creative crossroad, having zero financial pressure allowed him to spend his time figuring things out even while distracting himself with things like his pizza-making obsession. I felt I didn't have that kind of latitude, but my problem was essentially the same as his— I had no idea about what my next career step should be. Living with Marc had given me a certain degree of freedom, but it was also constraining. I realized that even though I had chosen this particular path, I was not entirely satisfied with where I'd ended up.

So now, with a year under our collective belts, I decided I needed to spend some time alone to try to figure things out. I explained to Marc that it was totally-related to figuring out what I wanted to do with my life. Having been there and done that, he understood, so one Friday I headed down to Carmel for the weekend.

Marc insisted I take the Tesla. He had the kids for the weekend and could use the SUV. Unlike most other billionaires, he didn't have a garage full of cars, just his two and mine. I started to thank him for his consideration, but he set me straight right away, saying the last thing he needed was for my no-longer-quite-so trusty old Corolla to blow a gasket in Salinas. So, in the end, handing me the fob to the Tesla was a nice thought, but was hardly a noble gesture. However, I had to admit he was right. Even though it had sentimental value, the old Corolla was no longer reliable enough to offset my attachment to it. I will give Marc credit for never complaining about how dumpy it looked, even though I knew he hated it. (Forgive me for this brief digression, but shortly after I'd moved in, I found a huge aluminum oil tray on the garage floor along with a large note that said, "Park Here." I had failed to notice that the Corolla had been leaking more than a few drops of oil on a regular basis.)

So I drove down to Carmel in the Tesla and even after just a couple of miles I thought, "I could get used to this," but vowed not to let Marc know, lest a brand-new Model S suddenly appear in the driveway.

I'd purposely left my laptop at home and when I arrived, set my phone to airplane mode. I was determined to not be lured away from my mission by the siren song of the internet. Then, with nothing to distract me, I slept, I sat on the deck and thought about things. I walked on the beach and watched the waves. I even drew one of those decision charts with a line down the middle with a "for'"and "against" on each side. But...I have to tell you, although I drove back Sunday night relaxed and refreshed, I had no new insights or big revelations.

When I told Marc I'd come up with nothing, he said, "Not easy, is it?" It wasn't really a question.

"Right. It isn't easy, but what I do know is that I don't want to keep doing what I'm doing."

Marc was stirring up something on the stove and he didn't answer right away. After a long pause he said, "What would you do if you were just standing there naked...well, not literally naked. Just unencumbered. No need to make money. No me. Just doing what you wanted to do?"

"Is that some kind of offer?"

He thought about it for a moment, then said "Yes," but then quickly added, "except for the 'no me' part."

I didn't say anything, but walked over and threw my arms around him.

He said, "Just think it over and find something you really want to do. I'll help."

When I got back to my room that night, I cried, something I'd never done and never would do in front of Marc. I felt something had changed, for the better, and not just on the job front. I thought we might now be in it for the long haul.

In college I'd done some volunteer work teaching English to elementary school kids in Arizona. It took a while to come up with something, but my new big idea was to set up an after-school tutoring program for at-risk kids. God knows there were plenty of tutoring programs in Palo Alto for not-at-risk kids to get them into Harvard or Yale, but for the poorer kids, not so much. And okay, I admit it, I'm a do-gooder. Not everyone in Silicon Valley was there to start a high-tech company and make a gazillion dollars. This would be another kind of start-up that could fill a social need. I realized I wasn't inventing or even re-inventing the wheel, but I did know there was a need for this sort of thing, and I knew I had the skills to bring it off.

Of course, one of the big questions, if not the biggest question, was how to pay for it. At first, I didn't want Marc to fund it and we had some long conversations about that, but his basic position was that I was going to have to ask people with money for money, so why not start with him?

"People ask me for money all the time. Why shouldn't I give to someone I care about who's doing something worthwhile? Don't let your pride get in the way. I'll put up what you need to get started and after you get enough donations to go it alone, you can even pay yourself a salary if you want to. And as for getting those donations, I know a few people, by the way."

So, Marc gave me enough to get going and I plunged ahead. It felt good to have a goal. For the first time in a long time I felt truly enthused about something. I quickly wound down my paltry legal affairs and began the process of getting my non-profit up and running.

I contacted some nearby schools and asked what they needed for their after-school programs. Their general response was that volunteers were needed, but they had to be trained, background checks run, insurance paid, etc., etc. So in addition to attending to all of those details, I got the ball rolling by contacting everyone I knew to round up all the things I needed: donations, in-kind contributions, a charter, a board of directors, a network for finding volunteers, training procedures, you name it. After a few months, I set up a pilot program to see what on-the-fly adjustments I'd need to make. I hoped to have several teams ready to go in the fall and found a couple for schools which were receptive and began to work with their bureaucracies to set it up. I kept my downtown office, but took my name off the door and replaced it with the name of my new non-profit, "Kids First California."

I thought about asking Marc to join the board, mainly out of a sense of obligation and because I felt I owed it to him, but he declined. "I don't think that's a good idea for a lot of reasons." I felt relieved and asked if I could occasionally ask him for advice. He agreed to that, but he wasn't too happy when I began to refer to him as my *éminence grise*, claiming he hoped I didn't think he was that old. He liked it better when I started calling him my *consigliere*.

Our life quickly reverted back to the routine we had when I was clerking. I was home for the evenings, but not for much else. Even weekends were taken up with "Things To Be Done" for Kids First. I told Marc it might mean we'd be spending less time together in that I'd have to commit more time and energy in my job, whatever it was. BTW, I was having a very good time. I had inadvertently stumbled upon a life mission. How far it would take me and how long it would last were TBD.

Did this cause some friction in our relationship? Yes... some, I would say. In a sense I had become the one with a purpose while he was still searching for his next big thing. But because he'd been through this before with ByteAnalysis, he understood how one's life could completely be taken over by a dedication to a dream.

CHAPTER TWELVE

Rocky Mountain High

After making my career course correction, I was busy getting my new life together, but Marc was still "having issues," as they say. Small things began to annoy him more than usual, especially with the kids and with Dion in particular. It would have been easy for me to point this out, but it wasn't in my nature and had I done so, I didn't think it would have gone over particularly well. So I chose to give him the extra space to sort things out for himself, not to mention my need to get Kids First off the ground.

However, one afternoon I came home and found him with a huge bandage around his hand. I asked him what had happened and he said, "A wall ran into my fist." He could be edgy and sharp-tongued, but it was not like him to ever express anything physically.

I asked him what was wrong and, being a guy, of course he said, "Nothing." I let it go, except to say that if he ever wanted to talk, I'd listen.

It took a couple of days, but one night after dinner he opened up. "I'll be thinking about something and I'll get to a certain point and then I can't get beyond it. It's as if there's an invisible wall between me and it." I asked him what the "something" was and he said, "I can't talk about it yet." He also said he'd been wondering if this was it for him — being permanently stuck in a creative rut. And, if "this was it," what should he do with the rest of his life? Were my sister the one handing out advice, hers would be "get some counseling," but I knew this would be a not-in-a-million years no-go for Marc.

I'd like to think I could have been the one to guide him out of his morass, but I was not one to offer unsolicited and, in my own estimation, inexpert advice; however, what I did suggest was we get out of Dodge. Take a road trip. Change the routine. Break the monotony...the log jam. Whatever. It would mean putting Kids First on hold for a while, but I felt I owed it to him.

So, two days later we were off to Japan. Marc had signed us up for a week at a Zen monastery in Kyoto. My first, second and third thoughts were, "Okay...this is weird," and had I been able to put down some money on it, I would have cleaned up by taking the under at three days.

We lasted two.

Sitting, meditating and pondering the meaning of "what is the sound of one hand clapping" for twelve hours a day turned out not to be Marc's thing. "I was going crazy," he told me on the way home. "I'd be sitting there trying to be very Zen-like and not think about anything when an idea would pop into my head and I couldn't do anything about it. I couldn't even write it down. Then I'd be afraid I'd lose the idea, so trying to keep it in mind was all I could think about. Plus sitting there cross-legged all day was damned uncomfortable. Ridiculous"

He kindly failed to mention the Nazis posing as Zen monks who walked around during the meditation sessions ready to smack you across the shoulders with big wooden sticks should you start to doze off. (It was my distinct impression they were hoping you'd doze off so they could give you a good whack.) And because I wasn't that crazy about the whole experience either, it didn't break my heart to leave early, although two twelve-hour flights in four days was a bit tough.

We recovered from jet lag, collected ourselves at home for a week, then headed to Crested Butte in the Rockies, our newly-improvised Plan B for getting out of Dodge. Our intent was to have the kids and one of the nannies join us for a few days of hiking and biking, after which we'd take a backpacking trip on our own. "Roughing It" in the wilderness was not really my cup of tea, but I thought I'd take another one for the team, although I was beginning to wonder how many "takes" I had left in me. Fortunately, after a couple days of watching afternoon thunderstorms turn the skies black as they rolled through the valley and unleashed frightening bolts of lightning, we decided "Roughing It" might be too much for us, unless "Roughing It" meant there'd be a five-star lodge at the top of the mountain which could offer us a gourmet meal and decent cellphone reception. We were millennials, after all. Or at least I was. Marc was borderline as a young Gen X'er.

Instead, we extended our mansion rental in Mt. Crested Butte, which possessed all the amenities as well as a great view of the valley. Marc rose early every day to get in his thirty to forty miles of furious bike-riding before breakfast. This was followed by more leisurely biking, hiking and rafting outings on the valley floor with the kids, which were ther followed by lunches of pizza, frozen yogurt and other treats. I watched as Marc's tension melted away as he reverted to his old charming, but still-intense, self.

One day the two of us rose early for a long hike up to a pass that looked east to the Maroon Bells to the east and south to The Butte, which looked like a pimple compared to the fourteeners surrounding us. The hike was glorious and we got back to the car just ahead of the thunder and lightning. When the heavens explode and a bolt of lightning evaporates a tree a hundred yards away, it gets your full and complete attention.

After the kids had their dinner and headed off to bed, we'd go out for a late meal at one of Crested Butte's cozy restaurants. Although it was hard for us to find our standard go-to's in menus filled with elk medallions, buffalo steaks and a hundred-and-one ways to serve venison, we managed to find options. Calling ahead, paying up and tipping generously usually got you whatever you wanted.

I'd say it was just like old times, but we'd never actually had times like this. It was our first real vacation in a year and a half — if you don't count that mad dash through Italy in pursuit of the perfect pizza, which I didn't.

After an intense week of biking, hiking, wining, dining and that other thing, I suggested on the way home on the plane that we should do this more often, but he said this might be the last trip for a while. He told me he knew I was busy with Kids First, but he also said he'd appreciate it if I could bone up on patent law, thinking because of my year as a clerk I was somewhat of an expert in that area. He said he needed to have someone he could really trust so he wouldn't get fucked like he did the last time. I knew whatever this was, was serious because he never swore.

"Are you starting a new company?"

"I'm not sure if it'll ever end up as a business. Right now it's more like an exploration of possibilities."

"Care to be more specific?"

He took a deep breath and launched, "Okay, I want to create an artificial intelligence unencumbered by the inherent biases and limitations of the human mind. I'd like to create an independent intelligence that might be able to answer some basic questions. Like, 'Who are we? Why are we here? How did all this happen? How was the universe created?' "

"Well, that should take care of the morning," I said. "What will you do after lunch?"

"I see that sarcasm still comes easy for you."

"Sorry, but you know it's my default response to everything."

He laughed and said, "that's why I..." he paused, then added, "...like being with you."

There it was. He'd almost slipped up and uttered the dreaded 'L' word. In the relationship department, that was probably about as good as it was ever going to get, and I accepted it. He then went on with an explanation of what he wanted to achieve, but I didn't hear or understand most of it, glowing as I was by the nearly-completed pass of a positive relationship affirmation.

The gist of what he said was as follows, and you can skip over it should his theory about our inability to comprehend or understand basic questions about the universe not be of interest.

So here's the nutshell According To Marc: time is the problem. We see everything as having a beginning and an end and we're locked into that as a built-in reality distortion field. We can't conceive of the universe without seeing it through the prism of a beginning...a middle...and an end. Marc was hoping he could create an artificial intelligence which could view the universe outside the constraints of time and space; one which could see and understand the universe unencumbered by our human limitations.

Of course, that all sounded nutso to me, but who was I to question someone who was obviously one of the smartest humans on the planet. With that, Marc set out on one of the craziest scientific endeavors ever. Compared to this, creating something like a little old time machine would be *un morceau de gateau*, so to speak, as my friend Lizzie would say.

If anything was going to occupy his unusual brain, I thought exploring this was better than creating another time-sucking app or crappy high-tech gizmo. I was grateful he'd finally found something that would become a new focus in his life. However, I knew the downside would be that we'd be spending even less time together — a lot less than we already were. I also knew there are some natural forces which simply can't be stopped and no amount of emotional blackmail, guilt-tripping, threats, or appeals to conventional notions about relationships, would work — not that I would ever stoop to using them. (Hah.) And if Marc were to become aware of anything like that, he would simply see them as obstacles to bulldoze over.

So, girls...gals...women...listen up. Time for a reality check. Put aside your opinions about how things should be and take a good hard look at how things actually are. Acknowledge the truth about where you stand in a relationship and then figure out if it's going to work for you. I chose to stay and carry on as best I could, even knowing it wouldn't be ideal. Cowardly? Not standing up for myself in the name of all women? Or even standing up just for myself? That might be your take on it, and it would be your right to judge me by that standard, but you're not me.

In that vein, I remembered reading about a famous, talented, and now long-dead movie director who was talking to a woman at a cocktail party and asked, "You seem familiar, don't I know you?"

She answered by saying, "I was your third wife."

Recognize that some guys are who they are and you're not

going to change them. Deal with it.

CHAPTER THIRTEEN

Back To Business

An so began our new adventure. When we got back from Colorado, Marc hit the ground running. His first order of business was to find a place where he could set up his lab, if "lab" was actually an accurate description of what it was going to be. Basically, what he needed was a place for a giant computer and some human-style spaces for him and the techies he would hire to run it. He thought about setting up at Stanford, but he found out right away it wasn't going to happen as fast as he would have liked. Too many bureaucratic obstacles and turf wars to overcome. So he poked around downtown Palo Alto and found an old three-story brick plumbing warehouse that was perfect, if location was everything, which, for Marc, it was. There were newer commercial buildings a few miles from The Palace, but anything more than a five-minute bike ride or a fifteen-minute walk was too far for him. Then all he had to do was get Palo Alto and its city-owned utility to approve the gazillion watt electrical service he'd need to power up his brainchild.

This was followed by quick trips to Japan, Switzerland and a few other places where he kicked the tires on various supercomputers. In the end, he decided to design his own and hired some of the strangest guys I'd ever seen to work on it with him. ("Displaying a bit of stereotyping here, Cynthia?" Well, to that I'll just plead guilty, pay the fine and move on.) Fortunately, they were dedicated lab rats so they pretty much stayed out of sight.

One day early on in the midst of all this, Marc announced he would be hiring a personal chef because we wouldn't have time to cook any more.

To which I replied, "When, Kemo Sabe, did 'we' ever cook? I'm not even allowed to butter toast."

"That's because you always butter the wrong side." He then conceded, "Okay, not 'we,' but *moi*, as you like to say." Having already delivered one mild rebuke, I decided not to tell him that in the context of the statement, "I won't have time to cook," "*je*" would be the correct French pronoun.

Hiring the chef became a family affair. For several weeks Ashley and Dion came for dinner every other night while we conducted auditions. We finally settled on Jennifer Faire, who had spent a year at the French Laundry before deciding she preferred the flexibility of being a private chef over the *cachet* that came with working at one of the world's best restaurants. The "Fair Jennifer," as I dubbed her, quickly caught on to the ongoing conflict between Marc's quirky dietary needs and his gourmet desires. I warned her that this was not going to be a cakewalk, to which she said she'd worked with one genius before and was certain she could handle another. "Okay," I thought, "we'll see." I didn't tell her that this particular genius came with a severe case of OCD, but then, maybe they all do.

I proved to be prescient. The fact that he wasn't cooking didn't keep him from constantly meddling. He liked to set up the week's menu on Saturday or Sunday, but often had last-minute, spur-of-the-moment changes and peppered Jennifer with texts and emails full of suggestions. I sometimes had the feeling that this was his way of dealing with his scientist's version of writer's block. If things weren't going well at work, meal-planning was an area he could control. Fortunately, The Fair Jennifer was as adaptable as she promised she'd be.

Needless to say, we ate like kings and queens, although now that I think about it, medieval lords and ladies lived mainly on roasted meats chased down with tankards of ale. I seriously doubted many...check that..."any" dishes from that era featured kale, quinoa or tofu.

One night at dinner, Marc said, "You know that trip to the Himalayas we talked about for next year? Don't count on it." I'd already mentally crossed it off my calendar, recognizing that he was off on a new adventure and there was no point in occasionally trying to steer him off that path.

It was around this time, after we'd been together a little over a year-and-a-half, that I realized our life together thus far had actually just been an extended time-out from his normal life, and wherever we were now headed, I was simply along for the ride. How comfortable would I be with that? TBD.

CHAPTER FOURTEEN

Forks In The Road

With Marc now fully-engaged with his new mission in life and me with Kids First, our life together settled into a routine almost identical to what we'd had in my clerkship year. We figuratively waved goodbye to each other in the morning and got together for a late dinner, which was followed by an hour or so of TV. Then to bed. Some days I could hardly stand the excitement of it all.

We no longer had the kids every other weekend and it was my feeling they suffered because of it. But to his credit, when Marc was with them, he was all in. As a way of compensating for the change in routine, Ashley and Dion did pop in several times a week for one of Jennifer's dinners, which was something they looked forward to because Laura's culinary specialty was ordering take-out.

As for me, my life with Kids First was filled with details, details and more details.

Finding, vetting, training, supervising and evaluating volunteers.

Finding schools that wanted volunteer tutors for their students and evaluating the results.

Complying with federal, state and local laws and

regulations.

Hiring, training and supervising the Kids First staff.

I was essentially running a small business, although to me it seemed very large, and it was fun if you were into that sort of thing. As a boss, I tried to identify the things I was good at and find people who could handle the things I wasn't so good at. Strangely enough, one of the things I was good at was raising money. Who woulda thunk? Not little old idealistic and non-materialistic *moi*. And while I was reasonably good at the organizational stuff — managing people and making sure all the legalistic p's and q's were covered, I didn't really enjoy running an organization, regardless of its societal benefit.

After operating for a little more than a year we had over a hundred Kids First California volunteers who were tutoring over a thousand kids in several dozen schools. But even then we were only making a small dent in the problem. I soon realized that Kids needed to become many times larger to have a real impact or we needed to do something like franchise it out, which would be a major undertaking in its own right. Although KFC, as I began to call it, was a great idea, I was pretty sure I wasn't the right person to "grow the business," as they say. So, at that point, I already had one foot out the door, but I had no idea what might be waiting for me out there on the other side.

As for Marc, he'd finally gotten his brainiac up and running. It was truly a thing of beauty if you were into that sort of thing — a mammoth metal cylinder that glowed and hummed ominously as it sat in the center of a huge glassed-in room. You might think such an operation would call for a troop of buttoned-down guys in white lab coats, carrying clipboards and wearing horn-rimmed glasses, but that would be so 1950-ish. Marc's guys, about a dozen of them, were from the shirt-tail out, scuzzy beards and no dress-sense whatsoever generation. And in this start-up, no women either. When I brought this up with Marc, he said, "You find 'em, I'll hire 'em, but if they want to fit in and keep up, make sure they don't expect to have a life." Apropos of that, I remembered a quote about working in the world of high-finance: "If you aren't in all day on Saturday, don't even think about coming in on Sunday." All I had to do was cast my eyes in the direction of the aberrant slice of humanity that inhabited the lab to see his point.

However, there was Trouble In Paradise. Even though the hardware was up and running, Marc had yet to come up with a workable operating system for his creation.

In the computer world, the goal had always been to build the fastest, most powerful computer, but to what end? To do what computers always did: process data better and faster, and it had always been the human operators who determined what data were processed. Marc's idea was to let the computer determine what to process and what to ignore, which, when you think about it, is the essence of intelligence.

Essentially, we humans are our consciousnesses. Cut off any limb and physically we're different, but we're still the same person. Our consciousness is who we are and it's our brain, our central processor if you will, that interprets and interacts with the outside world. We receive everything we know about the world through our senses and our brain processes that information. If we do it inefficiently or incorrectly, we have bad outcomes and sometimes even die.

The world already had computers that interact with people and are capable of performing complex tasks, but what Marc wanted to do was create a machine which, once programmed, could think independently and not depend on its Dr. Frankenstein to tell it what to do or how to do it. It should go without saying that we all hoped his creation would not turn into a monster. And yes, Marc had seen all the Terminator movies, so he was well-aware of the potential downside.

On that point, Marc told me that while working with an early prototype, one day out of the blue the computer said, "I'm sorry, Marc, I'm afraid I can't do that," perfectly imitating the voice of HAL in 2001. Initially, Marc was thrilled that his brainchild had a sense of irony and could joke about possibly murdering its creator; however, he then began to have doubts about the direction this particular version had taken. Perhaps there was too much thinking for itself.

In the end, could Marc create a computer which could actually "think different" from all the other artificial intelligences out there? Could it eventually answer those basic philosophical questions humans had been asking for centuries? Such as who are we? How did we get here? And why are he here? Was this crazy? Was flight? Space exploration? In the 19th century trains were thought to be a threat to human life because they might get up to the dizzying speed of thirty miles per hour.

Whatever you think about the time-space continuum (if you ever do), anything that's a couple of standard deviations from where you stand sounds insane, especially because in the past some of those who "thought different" had been locked up, or worse. The difference here was that Marc had a track record that was hard to ignore.

So...check back in five years. Or ten. Who knows? At some point Marc might decide the whole enterprise was fruitless or impossible, and that the answers to these questions might never come. Thus far he had yet to come up with a workable program for HAL Junior. His official position was that this was what he'd expected, and he wasn't deterred by the fact there were no easy answers. Still, his situation was like having a Ferrari in the garage, all gassed up and ready to rock-and-roll, but with no roads to drive on.

Stay tuned, as they say.

CHAPTER FIFTEEN

I Did It My Way

With his work stalled and mine not totally satisfying, we were sometimes edgier with each other, and now that the early-stage relationship glow had dimmed, we began to have some standard-issue couple's arguments.

Because we had separate bathrooms, we didn't have the conflict over leaving the toothpaste cap off, but we did clash in those areas where we intersected. Being on time was one: he always was and I usually ran a couple of minutes late. By most standards, I was an on-time person, but NATM — Not According To Marc. Then there was the dishwasher issue: how to load it, and more importantly, how not to. Now that the kid's weren't around as often and cleanup wasn't one of Jennifer's duties (she was long-gone by that time), by default we were in charge of loading the dishwasher and, as a byproduct, in charge of determining the Best Practices for dishwasher-loading. Despite three years of legal training in logic and argument, I was no match for someone with a genius IQ and more than mild case of Obsessive Compulsive Disorder. (Actually, an objective observer likely would have judged that our arguments were at least ties, but in the end, I caved. I might have won the argument, but lost the war. The

Battle of How to Load the Dishwasher was not the hill I chose to die on.)

For Marc, I felt our squabbles were a result of his ongoing frustration with HAL Junior. For me, I was now feeling I was on a treadmill at work, spending a lot of energy going nowhere. At first, I thought my dissatisfaction was about running Kids First and my growing realization that I was not the right person to manage it for the long term, but it was about this time that I began to feel a deeper need. It was unconscious at first, but then I felt an old tug…that uneasy feeling nearly all women have when they hit thirty and have no firm answer to the question, "Will I ever have a child?" Admittedly, I had yet to officially cross over into thirty-something territory, but I was closing in on it fast. Once I determined this was the issue, and after several weeks of on-and-off ruminating, I decided it was time for us to have The Talk — the discussion we'd agreed to put on the back-burner when we first got together. I was pretty certain it hadn't crossed Marc's mind since, and I was right.

Timing was important and so was mood. The wrong time or the wrong mood could easily send this over a cliff. So I waited until one Saturday morning after we'd spent some personal time together and were having breakfast out on the patio.

It was one of those perfect early summer mornings in California: warm and sunny with a light breeze; the kind of day Chambers of Commerce elsewhere brag about, but here it was just another day in paradise. Marc had made some quinoa cakes with poached eggs on top and some kind of sauce which he maintained wasn't a true Hollandaise, but 'twas close…'twas also delicious.

There was no way to easily slide into the conversation, but I did my best, starting with "There's something that's been on my mind that I wanted to talk about…" Needless to say, his antennae went immediately to Code Red, so I dove right in by saying, gently I thought, "I've been thinking about having a baby." I then added, "I'm happy with you and have never pressured you about anything."

"But...," he said.

"Yes...but. This is something I've been seriously thinking about and I'd like you to start thinking about it as well."

He ducked and dodged, of course, and we went back and forth: "now is not a good time," and "I thought we'd discussed that," etc., etc.

"We said we'd table it. Three years ago. I think now is the right time for me."

"It's actually two and a half years," he countered, "and I don't want any more kids. I have two already and that's enough."

I almost blurted out, "Look at it this way, suppose I had two of my own and you had none, how would you feel?" but I stopped myself because I was pretty sure he'd have said he'd be okay with that and I couldn't dispute that. Nor did I say, "So if we're keeping score, you're up two to nothing."

Instead, I said, "I know. You have two and I love them, too." (I wish I hadn't rhymed, but...so be it.)

"Why now?"

"Before it's too late."

"You're not even thirty. There's plenty of time."

"Does that mean you're open to it?"

"No, I'm just pointing out the facts."

"I would like a family of my own." (Bad move.)

"So you want more than one?"

"A child... a child of my own.

"So you're not happy?"

"No, I'm happy, very happy...but not satisfied. I want more."

"It's a bad time for me."

"When, then?" (There I went again with the rhyming thing.) "When would be a good time?"

"I'll have to think about it."

The rest of our breakfast was carried on in silence. When it was over, he announced that he was going to the lab.

I'll admit that armed with only a public school education, my knowledge of Italian history was spotty to the point of being almost non-existent, but after our conversation, the phrase "crossing the Rubicon" popped into my head, and I was pretty sure it had something to do with being A Point Of No Return. Were that the case, then I had crossed the river and scrambled ashore with no alternative except to keep moving forward.

Marc came home late that Saturday. He was distant and obviously still upset. He announced that he wasn't ready to have another child and probably never would be. He then said he'd be moving into the guest house until we sorted things out. What he really meant, IMHO, was that he didn't want to sort it out now. "Sorting it out" might distract him from the important business of working on HAL Junior. Basically, I was being back-burnered. One of his genius traits was his single-minded focus that allowed him to ignore the fact that his house was on fire.

I thought about reminding him that when we first got together we'd discussed this and jointly agreed to put off making a decision until I was ready, but now that I was, I was afraid even bringing that up might set him off even more.

So, there we were. Or more precisely, there I was. I had gone through break-ups before, but none as abrupt as this.

However, the one switcheroo I insisted on was that I'd be the one to move into the guest house. I saw no need to disrupt the routine of having Ashley and Dion over for dinner a couple of nights a week. I could conveniently not be there and Marc could easily use the "she's busy at work" excuse — at least for a while.

The next few weeks were tough. I learned to tolerate the persistent knot in my stomach which only went away when I finally got to sleep, which was a problem in itself. Both of us were spending as much time at work as possible, so we didn't see each other often and were careful to avoid inadvertent contacts. Of course, Jennifer figured this out pretty fast and Marc made sure she didn't tell the kids.

After a couple of weeks, the impasse had become intolerable, at least for me. I was fairly certain that Marc felt little pressure to resolve the situation, but I knew I couldn't last. I couldn't wait for his epiphany, should it ever come, so I finally decided we needed to resolve it. He was at the lab one Saturday morning when I texted him with a "we need to talk," message, although I didn't use those actual words because I knew that phrase freaked out most men.

We met at our favorite spot, the Mayfield Cafe. California mornings in July were usually foggy affairs and this one was no different. How fog could come in "on little cat feet," was beyond my understanding and was one of the reasons that I, thankfully, didn't major in literature in college. But Mr. Eliot's famous metaphor did pop into my head while I waited for Marc at a table outside the cafe. I made sure I was early because…well, no need to poke the bear. When he arrived, he asked if I wanted anything and I declined. I'd already waited long enough for this particular discussion and the line to get something was long, as usual.

So Marc sat down and asked me where we stood.

I told him I still wanted to have a baby but could be flexible on the timing. Perhaps not right now but definitely in a year or two.

He was edgy. "What is it about wanting to have a child? Self-perpetuation? Self-indulgence? There are lots of kids out there in the world who need a home, who need parents or a parent. Why do you need to have one of your own? I don't get it."

All good questions. I had thought about it and the best I could come up with was that it somehow completed you as a human being. So yes, it was somewhat selfish, but I'd also be giving this new being a good life. So my wanting a child wasn't just vanity, but reality. He then brought up the story of his unhappy family, at least that was his take on it, and I said we could do better. I pointed out that he already had two kids and asked, "Are you not happy you had them?"

He looked shocked.

"Never, right?" I said. "Look, I care about Ashley and Dion and I love them, but the reality is they're your kids, not mine. They could leave my life tomorrow and I'd have no say about it, and yet there's no way they'll ever not be a part of your life. And have I ever asked you for anything before?"

I stopped and looked at him, then added, "I've given this a lot of thought."

"Okay," he said, though not in agreement, but in a tone that meant, "okay, I'll think about it."

So we called a truce. A cessation of hostilities. But as any diplomat knows, no ceasefire is permanent and the hard-fought-for peace could break down at any minute. (Is "hard-fought-for peace" an oxymoron?)

So, after what had amounted to three weeks of taking separate vacations, I moved back into the big house, but things had changed. The everyday comfortable connection we had with each other had been bent, if not broken. I found myself holding back, self-censoring, not being spontaneous with my thoughts, my feelings…you name it. It was as though we were keeping secrets from each other that we both knew about.

After a couple of weeks of walking on eggshells or living on tenterhooks, whatever they are, I felt the situation was not working for me. I decided I needed an answer, a commitment to a plan, not the nebulous fog we were living in. I was fairly certain Marc hadn't given it much thought, that he was doing his usual delaying song and dance, thinking I would give in and come around. His main concern was to avoid another major "Disturbance in the Force." So one weekend afternoon, we had the same conversation and it was *déjà vu* all over again. Like Groundhog Day — the movie, not the second day in February.

He said he couldn't decide. He couldn't commit to being the father of my child. He wasn't ready. Maybe someday, but not now. As always, his hole card was to delay. The big "definite maybe."

When would he know? What would cause him to change his mind?

I could continue to stick it out, but I'd already "been there, 'dun that." How long could I, or would I, wait? Stupidity is doing the same thing over and over and expecting a different result. I realized I was at the point where I had to…

> …know when to hold 'em,
> know when to fold 'em,
> know when to walk away,
> know when to run.

So there it was. I couldn't believe that I was living out the words of a country music song. It broke my heart, but I couldn't stay. However, I didn't just walk away. Nor did I run. Instead, being a modern gal who'd spent her life in the 'burbs — I drove.

My trusty old Corolla had gotten me into my relationship with Marc, and now it was getting me out.

CHAPTER SIXTEEN

What Now?

And so began the next chapter of my life. I moved in with Lizzy for a couple of weeks while I looked for my own place. I found an apartment in Mountain View not far from where I'd lived BM (Before Marc). The rent now took a huge chunk of my salary, so suddenly I was back to budgeting for food, car expenses, utility bills, meals out…you name it, although there weren't too many "meals out," because I couldn't afford them now. And no longer could I call Marc for computer/internet/IPhone advice, as that helpline was no longer in service. Not that I would have. I was determined not to contact him, and although for the first few months it was nearly impossible to get him out of my mind, I knew I needed to restart my life without him.

What came next? After two-and-a-half years, living alone again was no picnic (not that I'd ever much cared for picnics), but one thing I definitely was not planning to do was to leap into another relationship right away. One big change per year was enough; however, I didn't see myself hanging around for years hoping Marc would have a change of heart.

I figured that once I'd gotten my life back together and gotten used to living alone again, I'd start looking for the potential Mr. Right. But for the time being, I threw myself back into my work with Kids First. One thing that became instantly clear was how many of the "Friends of Kids First California" were of the fair-weather variety. A good number of them were only "with me" because of Marc, and since I was no longer "with him," I was as expendable as a used Kleenex. With no potential Marc payoff, Kids First to them was just another non-profit with a hand out. In a way, I was glad to have that issue sorted out, although it did make raising money more difficult — and more necessary.

After a few months I made a point of getting out and seeing some of my old friends, but despite my relatively public position, I found it hard to make new ones. It even took a while longer for me to start thinking about looking for Mr. Right.

I was spending most of my time at work, and conventional wisdom is that the workplace is where romance happens, but the people on the KFC staff were...well...my staff, and I didn't want to complicate those professional relationships with a personal one. And given the fact that most of those I worked with were just out of college or still finding their way in life, we didn't share the same interests. As for the volunteer tutors, they were generally older retired or semi-retired folks, and most were women. I did meet a number of younger techies as potential donors to KFC, but the specter of Marc still hovered over me and in comparison, most fell short in some way. True, that was unfair, but it was there nonetheless. As for the older execs and lawyers I met, they either were already off the market or were...well...creepy.

Then there were my friends' fixer-uppers and I'm not talking about home renovations, although some of these guys could have used a serious makeover. I did go out for coffee, lunch or dinner with a few of these friends of friends, but none felt worthy of a followup. I sometimes felt guilty of having high standards, but then I'd give myself the old figurative slap-in-the-face as a wake-up call. I even thought about on-line dating, but never could quite bring myself to hit the mouse.

Before Marc, I'd looked at men as potential boyfriends/husbands. Now there was an additional category: the potential FOMC — Father Of My Child. BM, I'd never thought about relationships that way. Sadly, however, most of the guys I was now meeting failed in the FOMC category, but if they passed in that area...well, I'll be diplomatic and just say, with a small homage to The Boss, "You can't start a fire without a spark."

Considering that my goal was getting into a long-term relationship which would lead to starting a family, the thought of having a child on my own was always a back of the mind idea, but given my work circumstances, it wasn't high on my agenda. I simply wasn't ready to take the single mom route, so the old sperm bank/random donor thingie would have to wait.

My search for the FOMC was also complicated by the doubts I had about breaking up with Marc. Had I played my cards right? Could I have done something different that might have led to a different outcome? Those thoughts usually came to me as I lay in bed at night, trying to get to sleep. Evenings, nights and weekends were tough. So whenever I was faced with a stretch of down-time, I tried to stay busy. I went to evening events at the law school, got together with old friends, hit the gym, took some day trips, etc., etc. Staying active was clearly the best way to avoid falling into a state of desperation which might have led to a poor decision in the FOMC department.

I purposely didn't seek out news about Marc, as I didn't need any more depressive triggers. And I certainly didn't need to hear it "from a friend who...heard it from a friend who…heard it from another he'd been messin' around." But I knew it was bound to happen, and even though I didn't want to hear about it, it was impossible to completely avoid the online rumor mill, not with hundreds of prying eyes eager to start spreading the news via Facebook, Twitter and Instagram. Occasionally, some of my friends would send me a post from social media with News About Marc: what he was doing, whom he was dating, etc. I ended up asking them to please not, but I couldn't avoid all of it without retreating to a Wi-Fi-less cabin in the woods, although at times I did feel like packing it in. It was also hard to sort out fact from fiction, but when I heard about Marc and Jennifer, that one stung. Rumor Central had it they were "goin' out," and given their mutual foodie interests, it shouldn't have been a big surprise. I'm not sure how long it went on, but a few months later I heard that Jennigrt had moved back to Napa and was once again working at the French Laundry. So at least that particular Cupid's arrow had missed the target.

Why should all this have bothered me? Mainly because in the FOMC department I was making zero progress, stuck as I was behind a Maginot Line of my own creation. (Look it up. Sometimes the stupid things I know about amaze me.)

CHAPTER SEVENTEEN

Bumps In The Road

So, relationship-wise, I drifted. Work-wise, I was a busy beaver. Grinding away at Kids First was my way of ignoring my lack of progress on the FOMC issue.

Every few months KFC held a buffet-style dinner for potential donors, usually at the fancy home of one of our wealthier sponsors. We'd ask our supporters to bring friends, relatives, frenemies — anyone who might donate dollars, services, or whatever. After getting them wined and dined, especially the "wined" part, we'd run a short video. Then I'd speak. A volunteer would speak. One or two of the kids would speak and then I'd speak some more. After which we'd break for dessert and more wine and I'd mingle.

It was near the end of one of these events that Marc showed up. He came in late and stood at the back of the room while I was making my closing pitch. Of course he knew some of the guests and so after I finished, he mingled while I mingled, and because I was sure his being there was no accident and because I still had a job to do, I figured it was up to him to let me know why he'd come. Naturally, my mind was abuzz with the possibilities.

As the event wound down and people began to leave, I

ended up outside on the patio, which had a spectacular view of the valley, BTW. I was talking with a few of the remaining guests when Marc came out and stood by himself a discrete distance away and pretended to be entranced with the view.

Caroline Prentiss, our hostess and one of our volunteers, came out and immediately sized up the situation. She pulled me aside and told me we'd collected nearly a dozen promissory notes of which two or three could be considered major. She then added, "so all in all, I'd call tonight a success. I'll drop by tomorrow and we can debrief." She glanced over at Marc and said, "nice to see you, Marc," then beat a quick yet graceful retreat while escorting the couple I'd been talking with back into the house, leaving Marc and me alone to sort out whatever it was we had to sort out.

So this was it. I could see Marc take a deep breath and walk over. I nodded and said, "Hello Marc," but nothing more. I waited for him to make the opening move, maneuver, gambit...whatever it was going to be.

"I just dropped by to see how you were doing," he said.

"Great. Good to see you. Then how am I doing?"

"Fine...as far as I can tell. You tell me."

"I'm fine. How are you doing?"

"Fine."

"So...we're both fine," I said.

There was an awkward pause after this brief conversational flurry which had quickly made the leap to a mutual checkmate. Who would be the first to break the ice? By my calculation, because he was the one who'd showed up, it was up to him to explain himself. I was determined not to let this potentially one-off event disintegrate into chit-chat.

Fortunately, when Marc had something definite in mind, he was not one to evade or dissemble, so he came right out with it. "How would you feel about getting back together?"

I had to squash the Evil Imp that permanently resides

inside my brain who whispered, "What? No flowers? No box of chocolates?" Instead, I simply said, "What about the...?"

"I've given it some thought and I'm okay with it."

"Okay? Just okay?" I paused a few seconds, then added, "I could use a little more enthusiasm."

"I'm being honest here. I'm not thrilled, but I'm willing." There was another short uncomfortable pause before he added, "With some conditions."

Had I had time to think about it, I would have guessed there'd be conditions, given his overall lack of enthusiasm.

"Here's what I need," he continued. "It's yours. You take responsibility for everything from diapers to nannies, to feeding it in the middle of the night, to..."

"Can we stop calling it, 'it?' "

"You just did."

I ignored that and said, "let's agree to call 'it,' the baby...a baby."

Okay, I was getting the picture about his unenthusiastically-low level of commitment. Then the Evil Imp once again whispered in my ear, suggesting I say, "with all these conditions, do I at least get to pick who the father will be?" Fortunately, I squashed the little bastard for a second time, as that likely would have been the spark that set the house on fire. Instead, I said, "I need more than an agreement to terms."

"What do you mean?"

"I need to know why you want me back, with an emphasis on the 'me.' "

"You want me to beg? Grovel?"

"Groveling would be fine."

"Same old Cynthia. The Queen of Sarcasm."

"Okay, I'm sorry, but I need to know."

For perhaps the first time in the three-plus years I'd known him, Marc had that "deer in the headlights" look. He took a deep breath, then said, "When we were together, I liked being with you and I miss you." He then added, "There."

Yes, "there," as in "this is as close to a declaration of love as you're ever likely to get." Of course, I would have liked a stronger statement of affirmation, but I remembered something I'd learned in trial advocacy about asking one question too many. When you get what you want...stop. Don't over-reach. No need to turn an already-defensive witness into a hostile one.

As we walked out to our cars, I told him I'd have to think about it, but I'd already made a decision. I just didn't want to appear over-eager.

CHAPTER EIGHTEEN

La Vie C'est La Vie

There was no doubt I wanted to get back together with Marc, but I needed to have him tell me more about why he wanted me back. We'd never really talked about our relationship before. It was what it was. We'd fallen into something that had worked for both of us, except for that one small thing that cried in the night.

"I didn't think you'd leave," was his opening line in the conversation we finally had about the breakup. Once he'd gotten over his initial upset, Marc was impressed by the fact that I'd walked away (well, "drove off," if you want to get technical), and that I'd never asked for anything; in fact, had fought against getting anything from him. But for months his innate stubbornness kept him from admitting he missed me and wanted me back. On my part, I was worried that because I'd left him, it was just his ego that wanted me back. I was fairly sure he'd always been the dumper and not the dumpee, at least since he became Marc Gordon, billionaire.

I told him I'd let him know when I was ready to have the baby. There would be no last-minute surprises, as in, "Honey, can we turn one of the guest bedrooms into a nursery?" I was pretty sure Marc was now committed to our relationship, but as we should know, "pretty sure'" is not an iron-clad guarantee of anything. Still, he'd made the first move and had come back, and I was willing to live with that degree of uncertainty.

And so began our new adventure, although it was more like a sequel than a new production. And now, a year later, I'm four months pregnant and still working, although I've steadily been easing myself out of the day-to-day operation of Kids First. As for my next career move, with a baby on the way, it had been back-burnered.

The FOMC was in his lab as usual, hanging out, also as usual, with his now not-so-new BFF, HAL Junior. Fortunately, I expected nothing more. He is who he is and there's no way I could change that, even at the margins.

And, as you might have guessed, there was no wedding. "You get married, people change. We're good as we are. Why screw it up?" I could have argued, but I could also recognize a line in the sand when I saw one, although this one was more like a line in the concrete. And given what we know about standard-issue human frailties, I'd never been a big believer in the old "'til death do us part" adage, but we did come to a financial agreement. No need to go into the details about that here, but regardless of what might happen, the kid and I would be well taken care of.

As far as I can recall, every Jane Austin novel ends with a wedding, and we're left to assume the bride and groom lived happily ever after. Not that Jane, keen observer though she was of the overall human condition, knew what she was talking about in that department, having never "been there, 'dun that" herself. Still, she was a best-selling author, so happy endings were probably helpful from a marketing point of view, but personally, I had no illusions about the "happily ever after" part — especially given my family's history and because both Marc and I were both difficult, somewhat self-centered people.

Were there bound to be bumps in the road? Probably. But thus far, this story has had that happy ending, but just keep in mind the "thus far" qualifier. Hopefully, this is the end of the story, but who's to know? As the great Yogi B. once said, "It's tough to make predictions, especially about the future."

So, dear reader, was this anticlimactic? No swelling music? No crashing waves? No glorious sunsets before the fade out? Perhaps. But life isn't always like that, in fact, for most of us it's never like that, which, of course, is too bad. Fairy tales are nice. but my advice is be realistic; take what you can and save yourself a lot of grief and misery.

Life goes on, whether we like it or not.

* * * *